CW00867690

Moon Strings and Birthday Letters

Rebecca Roundtree Hartdegen

WESTBOW
PRESS®
A DIVISION OF THOMAS NELSON
& ZONDERVAN

WestBow Press books may be ordered through booksellers or by contacting:

WestBow Press
A Division of Thomas Nelson & Zondervan
1663 Liberty Drive
Bloomington, IN 47403
www.westbowpress.com
1 (866) 928-1240

ISBN: 978-1-9736-5835-1 (sc)
ISBN: 978-1-9736-5836-8 (hc)
ISBN: 978-1-9736-5834-4 (e)

Library of Congress Control Number: 2019903677

Print information available on the last page.

WestBow Press rev. date: 04/25/2019

To my wonderful family: I love you all
with every breath of my being.
Thank you for dreaming with me.
To God be all the glory.

Call to Me and I will answer you and tell you great
and unsearchable things you do not know.
—Jeremiah 33:3

Prologue

Isabella has a love for the Lord beyond measure, a love rooted in a compassionate desire for others to know of His goodness. Oh yes, she wears her faith on her sleeve for everyone to see. But make no mistake, that sleeve is wrinkled from the pain and heartache that only God's hand can smooth. You see, Isabella has been healing from grief and loss for many years. She never expected to lose seven people she held dear in just eight years, while losing more as an adult. Fear remains relentless in its fight to steal away her peace. A divine revelation that will open wounds deeper than the Grand Canyon is drawing near. Meanwhile the purpose of Isabella's pain can be understood only by first looking back and embracing a time filled with wonder, moon strings, and birthday letters.

On August 28, 1980, in New Orleans, Louisiana, Isabella entered the world. Around the age of five, she began hoping for a brother and sister. Around that same time, Isabella starting telling her parents that God uses three strings to hold the moon in the sky. The stars, as she explained, reflect off the moonlit strings and move with the breath of the Holy Spirit, and that's why they appear to sparkle. The three strings represent the Father, Son, and Holy Spirit—innocent wonder and childlike faith at their purest.

Five years later on Thanksgiving Day, Isabella's mother

gave birth to twins, Rowan and Eliza. A long-awaited wish had finally come true. Isabella gave her parents a congratulations card that she made with bright blue and pink construction paper. The handwritten message inside thanked God and her parents for making her a big sister. That night Isabella promised God that she would try to be the best sister ever.

Isabella's smooth sail through life became rough when deep grief entered her heart eleven months later with the loss of her grandpa. Oh, how she had loved him. Soon her parents began hearing her say, "I'm going to sit out on the deck." The wrought iron table and chairs outside served as her hiding place. One night while looking up at the star-filled sky, Isabella begged for answers. "God, you've never let the moon fall out of the sky. Couldn't you have used that same power to keep Grandpa from dying? I'm not trying to be mean, but why did he have to go home now? I love you, but this hurts."

In the kitchen, Isabella's parents happened to hear their daughter's prayer through the open window. Her father, whose heart was heavy from losing his father, turned to his wife and wept. Out of their pain, however, a purpose and healing balm would soon be unveiled at Isabella's thirteenth birthday celebration.

Waiting for guests to arrive, Isabella decided to go outside and sit on the deck for a few minutes, where her parents soon joined her.

"Princess, today is very special," said her father. "The next chapter of your life story starts today! A new tradition is in the making too. You're the first one—"

"So cool, Daddy! What's the tradition? Are you and Momma going to take me somewhere special?" Interrupting her father midsentence was classic Isabella. Eager to know what was inside the pink envelope her father was holding, she was all ears.

Her father went on to explain the tradition. Every year, all three children, between the ages of thirteen and twenty-one, would receive a birthday letter from him. "Sweetheart, when your mom and I are long gone, the letters will serve as reminders of the joy we had in watching you grow up. They will chronicle your life and how God moves in it—all your experiences wrapped up in the pages of my letters, to inspire you to never give up. Most of all, we want you to know how much you're loved and that no matter what happens, God is and will always remain faithful."

Looking at her parents, Isabella could sense this moment was quite special. "Okay, y'all are going to make me cry. Love you both so much. Can I read it now, or should I wait until the party?"

Her mother reached for Isabella's hand. "Whatever you want to do, sweetheart, is fine with us."

Just as Isabella stood to read the letter, the pink and white twisty strap on her right sandal got wedged in her chair. "Well, that was graceful," she exclaimed, laughing so hard that her parents joined in. "So, while we're here, want to know my birthday wish?"

"Bet your mom and I have a pretty good guess. Italy, right?" asked her father.

"Yep! I don't know how or when, but one day I'll go to Rome. I'll have my photo taken on the Spanish Steps to prove that I was there, and then I'll make a wish and throw coins into the fountain!"

Isabella's mom leaned over to hug her. "I really believe you'll go there one day, Bella. I really do."

Isabella decided to read the letter in front of everyone at the party. As she read aloud, the sound of sniffles echoed throughout the living room, so she knew that other people were as moved by the words as she was. If ever there was a moment that Isabella wanted to bottle up and save, it was her thirteenth birthday party.

Settling in later for a good night's rest, Isabella turned on her bedside lamp and read the letter again:

Princess, the clock of life is ticking much faster than your mother and I would like. The lullaby "Turn Around," sung by Malvina Reynolds, includes the words, "Where are you going, my little one?" This song, which I'm sure you've heard, tells about a parent's surprise at how quickly their daughter has grown—and that's how your mother and I feel. It felt strange to watch you leave for school this morning, knowing that we were watching our thirteen-year-old daughter go out the door. We have watched you go out the door to school for eight years, so we should be used to it by now. Where have all the years gone?

The song goes on to say, "Turn around, and you're a young girl." Your birthday is a time for us to turn around and see how much you've grown. You're a beautiful, bright, independent young lady of whom we are quite proud. Your mother and I are in a race with time, and we want to win. In the precious years between now and when you have babes of your own, we want to give you all the love, support, guidance, advice, and respect we possibly can. One day you will go out on your own, and we'll stand in the shadows and confidently watch you try out your wings. But before we

back away, we're going to do our best to let you know
that we are here.

Before she could finish reading, Isabella drifted off to sleep with the letter in her hand and hope in her heart.

Seven years have passed since Isabella last opened her memory box of letters. Tomorrow, on her twenty-eighth birthday, will be a good—and necessary—time to open the box again.

Chapter 1

"Dinner's ready, Isabella," Gloria announced as she placed linen napkins on the glass table decorated with a bright purple orchid. "There's a pitcher of sun tea I made in the fridge. Would you mind bringing it to the table?"

"Be right there, Mom," echoed Isabella's voice from the hallway.

Gloria, Isabella's mother, really knew how to cook. Her meals were a savory delight that no one ever wanted to miss, least of all Isabella. As her mother had prepared tonight's dinner, Isabella had followed the delicious scents to the kitchen and asked what was cooking. Shrimp and crawfish pasta, roasted broccoli, grilled corn on the cob, and a raspberry vinaigrette-dressed garden salad full of cherry tomatoes, cranberries, and apple slices, with buttered dinner rolls on the side—it was one of Isabella's favorite meals, and she couldn't resist grabbing a shrimp right off the stove. As the sheers hanging in the living room window moved softly with the evening breeze, the delightful aroma permeated the entire home. A good recipe must include love, and every meal that Gloria prepared warmed the soul.

They held hands to say grace. Isabella cherished such rituals because they made her feel connected to her mother and God every day. Saying grace reminded her that life was bigger than the food before her—it was about connections. After her mother finished saying grace, Isabella smiled and they released each other's hand.

Then Gloria picked up a plate to serve her. Watching her mother's hands arranging the food on her plate, Isabella knew to be grateful. One day, after her mother went to heaven, she wouldn't see those hands again, so she didn't want to waste a minute of her mother's selfless love. "Thanks, Mom. Everything looks great."

"You're welcome, sweetheart. Hope you're hungry. Meant to ask you, all packed yet?"

Isabella replied, "Still have some clothes to wash when I get back home. Then I'll be done."

"Good. Well, let me know if you need anything. I'm happy to help."

"I know, Mom. I just…" Isabella put down her fork and took a deep breath.

"What's the matter, sweetheart?" Gloria was trying not to intrude, but her eyes were filled with motherly concern.

Isabella knew she'd have to be honest. "I miss Dad. He always told me I would go to Italy someday. I wish he was here. Hard to believe it's been almost three years."

"I know, honey. I miss him too. Listen, how about some coffee? I just bought hazelnut creamer yesterday. Want some?"

"Ooh, that sounds good," said Isabella. "I'll get the cups. Coffee always tastes better here. Always." After visiting a bit longer, Isabella headed home.

Three months earlier, in May, Isabella had been notified that the Pulmonary Internship Abroad Program had accepted her application. Her dream of traveling to Italy was about to come true, and her life would be changed forever. Isabella had not originally set out to be a pulmonologist, but after watching her father battle chronic obstructive pulmonary disease and emphysema, she developed a desire to help other people who were going through similar experiences. Isabella had vivid memories of the oxygen tank that her father used to carry in a backpack, and she prayed every day to have courage like her parents. Every day.

After a house down the street had caught fire the previous week, Isabella had decided to take some of her nine birthday letters to Italy. That was also her way of taking her father along on the trip that he'd so often declared would come to pass one day. At first she couldn't decide whether to take the originals or copies, but finally she decided to take copies—just in case another fire destroyed her only tangible reminder of her father.

LifeSongs, Isabella's favorite radio station, was a much better alarm clock than the blaring and unwelcoming sound of *beep, beep*. Something about the uplifting worship music ministered to her spirit. Whenever she took one of her late afternoon drives by the lakefront, singing to her heart's content, Isabella was quite sure that the lyrics and the sunset were meant just for her. In those moments, all of her worries were washed away.

While Isabella was lying in bed enjoying the music, the previous night's dream came to mind. Out of the blue, it rushed in like the wind, and she wondered why she had dreamed about a wolf. Growing up hearing the Bible story of Joseph and his dreams, Isabella had always hoped that one day she'd be graced with the gift of visions like Joseph, and then be used by heavenly influences to bring those visions to pass. Recalling the image from her dream of the evil creature with its sharp teeth brought on chills. The wolf had threatened that if she dared to move, it would bite her and cripple her forever. With hands lifted high in the air, Isabella had prayed for God to remove her fear.

Trying to shake loose her memories of the dream, Isabella

got out of bed. It was her birthday, after all, and she was determined to enjoy every minute of it. As she tried to choose between a sleeveless light blue linen dress and jeans with a white frilly lace top, her phone rang.

"Hello?" said Isabella.

"Happy birthday, lady!" It was her mom, who was always the first to call on her birthday.

Isabella loved her mother for that, and even at the ripe old age of twenty-eight, she had been looking forward to that call. "Thanks, Mom!" she said. "Can you believe your firstborn is twenty-eight?"

"My goodness," her mother said. "Seems like yesterday I was putting bows in your hair."

Isabella agreed, "I know, doesn't it?"

"Hey, can you come over to the house a little early before we go to lunch?"

"Yes, I'll be there as soon as I figure out what to wear."

"Well, make sure to watch the time," her mother said. "We don't want to be late."

"I know, Momma. Don't worry. I'll be there."

"Okay, Isabella, see you soon. We'll have fun today!"

"Yes, we will. Now, let me go so I can finish getting dressed," said Isabella.

"Okay. Bye."

"Bye, Mom." Each moment counted to Isabella, and hearing the excitement and love in her mom's voice when she mentioned putting bows in Isabella's hair was precious. To Isabella, that was a moment not to be taken for granted—a gift in and of itself.

Seconds later, the phone rang again. "Hello?" said Isabella.

"Happy birthday, my friend!" Annalise's voice was cheerful, as always. She was one of the nicest people Isabella had ever known. A year earlier, Annalise had miscarried twins, and Isabella was amazed that through it all, Annalise had maintained her positive outlook.

"Hey, Annalise! Thanks for calling. Oh, and before you ask, I've already made a wish. He has dark hair and brown eyes."

Annalise asked, "Who does?"

"My birthday wish!" exclaimed Isabella.

"Girl, you're too funny."

"You never know, Annalise. It could happen, and when it does, you'll be the first to know."

"Oh girl, of course," said Annalise. "If there's anyone who deserves to meet a nice guy, it's you, my friend."

"Aw, thanks. So you're still coming to lunch with us today, right? Is Steven coming with you?" Isabella asked.

"I'll be there, but Steven has to take the kids to a birthday party at the trampoline place uptown. The kids made sure to pick out a special birthday present for you. Way too cute, Isabella. I'll bring it with me."

"So sweet," Isabella said. "Give them a hug for me."

"Will do," Annalise promised. "You know, Steven mentioned last night that he wants to start a birthday letter tradition too, when the kids turn thirteen. I wish your dad was here so I could tell him. He really inspired me so much. Can't wait to tell your mom that Steven has already started keeping a journal about the kids. It's precious."

"That's wonderful. Mom would love to hear you say that—I just know it. She's really missing Dad. Well, listen, I'm supposed to meet Mom at her house soon, and I still haven't decided what to wear!"

"You better hurry, girl. Bye!" said Annalise.

Almost ready to walk out the door, and wearing her new jeans and frilly white blouse, Isabella ran back to the kitchen to grab a bottled water. Closing the refrigerator door, she noticed a heart-shaped reflection on the hardwood floor, coming from the sunlight shining through the window. Looking at it for a moment, she couldn't help but think it was a wink from heaven.

With the radio up and the windows down, Isabella sang as loudly as she could, all the way to her mom's house. Turning into the neighborhood entrance with its double row of twelve oak trees always took her breath away. Something about those old oak trees reminded her that Jesus was the vine and she was a branch, an extension of His love meant to share truth.

As Isabella's car turned into her mom's driveway, the Bible on the front seat fell open. Turning off the car, she reached over to close the Bible and caught a glimpse of the words on the open pages. The passage in Revelation was about twelve fruits on the tree of life. Looking in the rearview mirror at the twelve oak trees behind her, she thought, *How ironic. Could God be trying to give me another message? Could this be a hint about my dream?* Her mind raced as she tried to piece together the scripture and the dream—the water, wolf, dry land, trees. Isabella didn't believe it was by chance that she had seen the scripture, and she smiled at the possibility of divine influence.

"Hi, Mom! I'm here," she called out excitedly, walking into her mom's house.

Isabella's mom walked into the room carrying a gift box wrapped in pink and purple paper with white ribbon. "Happy birthday, sweetheart! You look so pretty."

Isabella's shoulder-length, wavy, light-brown hair with fresh caramel highlights looked quite beautiful. With her slender five foot eight frame, Isabella looked like a model, but she didn't think of herself that way.

"Momma, you look so pretty."

"Do you really like my hair? Tell me the truth, Isabella. I let the stylist cut it really short this time."

"I really do," insisted Isabella. "You're gorgeous!"

Gloria said, "Well, it's sweet of you to say that. So listen, it's nice outside, so I thought you could open your presents out on the deck."

"Since we have a reservation, don't you think we should head out now?"

"I really want you to open it here, honey," insisted Gloria. "It won't take long."

"Okay, Momma, sounds good."

They walked through the white French doors onto the deck.

"Wait till you see the night-blooming jasmine, Bella."

"Momma, it's beautiful. A birthday bloom just for me. How 'bout that!"

There was no mistaking her mother's gift for gardening. The myriad colors—yellow, pink, white, red, lavender-blue, purple, and lilac—of the azaleas, petunias, hibiscus, crown of thorns, and wisteria plants were an eyeful. The sunlight seemed to dance on the petals. If color could be heard through musical tones, the deck plants were playing a classical symphonic masterpiece.

They walked over and sat at the table, and Gloria said, "Here's your present, sweetheart. Hope you like it."

"Oh, wow." That's all Isabella could say as she unwrapped the silver half-moon paperweight. The engraved message read, "Dreams do come true for all who believe." Moved deeply by her mother's thoughtfulness, Isabella gave her a bear hug.

Gloria said, "I thought you might like to keep it on your desk at the hospital. You were always talking about moon strings, God, and dreams. As soon as I saw it, I thought of you."

Isabella's voice cracked as she said, "It's lovely." Her heart melted at the thought that her mom had brought back a precious childhood memory of faith. Deep inside, Isabella was wrestling with the fear of leaving her mom to go clear across the world.

Gloria asked, "Do you remember asking us how many strings God used to keep the moon in the sky?"

"Yep, I do. You and Dad always told me that there were three strings, representing the fact that God holds yesterday, today, and tomorrow. Remember, I got three strings of yarn from your sewing box to make my own moon strings?"

"You were so cute, Bella, always talking about God's love," said Gloria. "You had no idea how much God was using you to encourage us. That was the night your dad and I found out that Grandpa was sick."

"All this time I never knew that, Momma. Wow, so I really encouraged you?"

"You sure did, honey. Never lose that childlike faith, Isabella."

"I won't, Momma. I promise."

"Well, listen, I have another gift for you." Isabella opened a white satin-wrapped box to reveal an exquisite triple-braided gold necklace with three small gemstones of purple, blue, and silver. Engraved on the clasp were the words "Wait on the Lord's favor."

"Momma, this is beautiful. I love it. Thank you so much."

Gloria said, "You're welcome, honey. See, I chose a triple braid to remind you of the Father, Son, and Holy Spirit."

"I love it, Momma. Hey, are you crying?"

"Oh, you know how sentimental I am," said Gloria.

"Yes, and I love that about you. Never stop being fabulous." Isabella reached for her mother's hand and pulled her to her feet, and they began twirling around like ballerinas. Isabella's heart was grateful to have such a kind and sensitive mother, and she didn't know what she was going to do without her in Italy for eighteen months.

Collecting herself, Gloria straightened her blouse. "Well, young lady, we'd better get going. Our reservations are in a half hour."

"Alrighty, I'll get my keys. Let's go have fun, Momma!"

"Sounds good to me!"

As she and her mom walked up to the restaurant, Isabella noticed balloons through the glass door. She was completely surprised to find Eliza inside, holding three balloons and a gift bag. Eliza held herself gracefully, as if she was about to leap through the air in a tutu. With her hair tied in a chocolate-brown bun neatly piled on top of her head, Eliza smiled with such sincerity that it humbled Isabella.

Isabella had thought that Eliza was at a student leadership conference in Florida, and she exclaimed, "Yay, you're really here!"

"When you left Mom's house after dinner," Eliza explained, "she went to the airport to pick me up. You had no clue, huh?"

"None whatsoever," Isabella admitted. "Good job!"

"So listen, when we visit you at Christmas, I want to throw three coins in the fountain like we saw in that Italian movie," said Eliza. "Remember, they made wishes and then threw coins in the water? I can't remember the name of the movie, but I remember that scene and we have to do that!"

"Count me in," agreed Isabella.

Their corner table provided a perfect view of the sailboats caressing the sun-kissed water, and Isabella snapped several pictures with her cell phone. She wasn't going to see the lake for a long time. Even worse, she wasn't going to see her family, and she already missed home.

Eliza handed Isabella the gift bag. "Here's a little something from me. Hope you like it!" Inside was a bottle of Isabella's favorite perfume and a silk scarf.

"Ooh, I love my perfume, and this scarf is so nice." Unfolding the silk scarf, Isabella couldn't help but notice the beautiful lilac print, reminding her of the scent of lilac growing in a field. As she wrapped the scarf around her, she was already imagining different ways to wear it.

"A little birdie told me this would be a great present, so enjoy!" Eliza then politely excused herself and headed for the restroom.

"Excuse me, ma'am. May I take your order?"

Isabella looked up, surprised to see Rowan standing next to her table. Over six feet tall and in great shape with hair already thinning, he reminded Isabella of their dad more and more.

"No way. Hey, little brother!" Jumping up from her chair, Isabella hugged Rowan with the tightest bear hug she could muster. She had thought that he was out of town getting settled in at college.

"Momma," she asked, "did you know that Eliza and Rowan were going to be here?"

"Yep, but it wasn't easy keeping this secret from you, young lady. I almost gave the surprise away this morning."

"All I can say is my family rocks!" Looking around the table, Isabella felt such peace. Having her family together meant everything to her. She was feeling sentimental and nervous about leaving for Italy, and being with them was proving to be the sweetest blessing.

Rowan picked up Isabella's menu. "I'm taking care of our bill today, sis. Order whatever you want, and don't look at the prices. That won't matter."

"Really?" asked Isabella.

Rowan insisted, "Of course."

"Thanks, bro. Can't decide. It all looks good."

Annalise walked in about fifteen minutes later with more balloons, presents, and a strawberry cheesecake drizzled with caramel and chocolate.

Isabella picked up a fork and tapped her water glass. "You know what? I have an idea. We're going to change things up. Let's have dessert now, before they bring our entrees. Life's too short, so I'm eating dessert first!"

A few minutes later, Brendan, a family friend, walked in. The first to notice him, Isabella ran over to him with open arms. "Hey, you! Thought I wouldn't get to see you before I left. When did your unit get back?"

"Last night. Rowan called me and said y'all were having lunch here today. Couldn't pass up the chance to see my favorite girl," said Brendan.

"You're a mess, Brendan! So glad you're here!" As a teenager, Isabella had had a huge crush on Brendan, whose dark brown eyes and broad shoulders had always made her heart melt. He had been her junior prom date, and the photo they had taken that night at school showed him towering over her at six foot four. Eventually they had decided that being friends was best, but somewhere deep inside, Isabella still wondered if one day they might be more than that.

They had a feast—shrimp and steak kabobs, lobster tails, crawfish pie, catfish, sweet potato fries, vegetables, and garlic bread. Plates were emptied, and Isabella's belly was full and her heart was happy.

After lunch they all headed back to Isabella's mom's house to play a few rounds of croquet, a cherished Cole family tradition. Brendan ran out to Gloria's backyard and started setting up the croquet course, letting everyone know that he was going to win: "Love hanging out with you guys, but not enough to let y'all win!"

Isabella replied, "Actually, if I remember correctly, I've won the last four games. Oh, wait a second. I might still have our scorecard in the garage. I'll be right back." She dashed away in search of said scorecard.

Through the garage window, Isabella could hear laughter. She paused to let the sounds of family and fun sink in, wishing that she could bottle that moment. But then she ran back to the backyard and called out, "Found it. Let it be known that in Daddy's handwriting, it reads that I won the last four games. So y'all better watch out!"

"Game on, sister!" Rowan announced, nodding. "Time for battle!"

Isabella said, "Thanks, everybody, for being here. This is one of my favorite birthdays. I wish Dad was here." Then she lifted her croquet mallet in the air and said, "I'm going to try to win for you, Daddy!"

After three games, of which Isabella won two, it was time to call it an afternoon. Brendan had to go meet his parents, so he hugged everyone goodbye and said that he was already looking forward to the next croquet game. Rowan and Eliza both needed to catch their flights within the hour, Eliza to the West Coast and Rowan to the East, so Isabella went with her mom to take them to the airport. Wishing everyone could stay, while knowing they really couldn't, Isabella made sure to let them know just how much she loved them. She was already planning to book their flights to Italy for Christmas.

Isabella was feeling protective of her mother, so before leaving for her own apartment, she checked that all the doors at her mom's house were locked. She was also looking into buying her mom a dog for protection. Before she left, Isabella gave her mom a huge hug and said, "Mom, this was a wonderful birthday. You're my best gift."

"Sweetheart, I love you," said Gloria. "Your heart is precious. Now go home and get some good rest. Tomorrow's a big day!"

With that, Isabella drove home with a light heart and high hopes. Soon she climbed into bed and settled in for her journal writing time. As her pen glided across the page, a text alert interrupted the silence: *Swoosh!* Not wanting to interrupt her quiet time alone with God, Isabella ignored the text. But there was that sound again: *Swoosh!*

Then the phone rang, and Isabella got a sinking feeling that something wasn't right. It was Annalise calling, and Isabella nervously picked up the phone. In her past experience, whenever someone called her late at night, it was never good news.

"Hey, Annalise. Is everything all right?" asked Isabella.

Annalise said, "No, it's Brendan. He's gone. His mom called my mom and told her."

Her stomach already in knots, Isabella asked, "What do you mean?"

Annalise began, "Brendan was involved in a four-car collision by the lake, and …"

In complete shock, Isabella dropped the phone and began to wail. Brendan had held a special place in her heart. She had often described him as "meeting people where they are" because of his welcoming way. He had never placed judgment or tolerated prejudice. Their youth group had nicknamed him "a warrior for Christ" one summer when he teamed up with local church leaders to start a homeless outreach ministry. Brendan had planned to attend seminary someday, and Isabella had admired him beyond measure.

Shredded to the core and holding tightly to her tear-drenched pillow, she finally fell asleep.

Chapter 2

Restless through the night, Isabella barely slept a wink. She just couldn't believe that less than twenty-four hours earlier, Brendan had been visiting with everyone and full of life—and now he was gone forever. Isabella's mind had raced all night, wondering who would pass away next. Haunted with the thought that something tragic could happen to her family while she was in Italy, her soul was anything but calm.

While Isabella was lying under the covers, a beam of sunshine burst through the bedroom window blinds, reflecting a heart shape through the tree leaves. Two days in a row of seeing hearts! She would normally be quick to delight at such a coincidence, but that wasn't the case today. Aching bones, mental fog, and a throbbing headache did nothing to help her get out of bed. Rolling back over, she was staying put.

Three hours later the doorbell rang, followed by loud knocking. Crawling out of bed and still wearing her pajamas, Isabella opened the door to find Gloria standing there.

"I can't go, Mom. Something happened."

"What's going on?" asked Gloria. "You're going to be late. Didn't you set your alarm clock?"

"Mom, stop!"

"Don't yell at me, young lady. I'm just trying to help you."

"Sorry," said Isabella. "I know. Just give me a second."

"Isabella, we've already paid for the flight. We can't get our money back this late in the game."

"I know. Just give me a second!"

Confused, her mother asked, "What has gotten into you? Where is this coming from?"

"Brendan died last night!" Collapsing in her mother's arms, Isabella wept.

"No!" exclaimed Gloria. "Please God, no." She held her daughter close as Isabella's sobs grew louder.

Isabella wouldn't be flying to Italy that day. Later that afternoon, they learned that the funeral would be in three days. After rescheduling her flight for the day after the funeral, Isabella crawled back under the covers. Cold chills ran down her spine at the thought of Brendan lying lifeless in a box, and her skin felt like it was crawling. Rowan and Eliza would be arriving the next day, and Isabella was glad they were coming, though not for such a sad reason.

On the day of the funeral, Isabella finally took off the pink cotton pajamas she had been wearing for two days and got in the shower. The hot water felt good on her cold skin. "Help me, Jesus, please," she prayed aloud. Wearing a black linen dress and long pearl necklace, she stared at herself in the full-length mirror. She felt scattered inside, and her nerves were on edge as she struggled to believe where she was going. A breakfast of strong coffee and toast was all she could manage as she waited for her family to pick her up.

As she walked to the door of the funeral home, a bright blue and purple butterfly landed on Isabella's right shoulder. "Maybe that's a wink from God, Momma," she said to Gloria.

"Maybe it is, sweetheart. Maybe it is." Gloria hugged Isabella tightly.

Holding the door open for them, Rowan added, "Nice thought, sis."

"Agreed," whispered Eliza, grabbing a tissue from her purse.

Listening to their pastor speak about Brendan's life moved Isabella's heart. God was being honored in the process, and Isabella knew Brendan would have liked that. At the service's end, the funeral home attendant advised that anyone wanting to go to the cemetery for the graveside service should go ahead and get in their cars. The pit in Isabella's stomach grew deeper. Right now she was close to Brendan and could still see him, but soon she would see him no more. She wondered what her last words to him should be.

The sun was shining brightly, and Isabella welcomed the warmth on her cold skin. Birds chirped rhythmically as if singing their own song of praise to the heavens. The moment came for people to say their final goodbyes. With head bowed, Isabella walked up to the coffin and whispered, "Until we meet again in heaven, my friend. I love you."

Gloria suggested they go back to the house, where she would prepare a pan of lasagna. Isabella still wasn't sure that she could stomach any food, but she was willing to try. She managed to eat about five bites and then excused herself to lie down on the living room sofa, where she fell asleep.

The next morning, Isabella woke up early. She could smell banana bread, bacon-and-cheese omelets, and a hint of coffee in the air, but she didn't have an appetite. Not even her regular routine of eating a heaping tablespoon of peanut butter in the morning was appealing, but she did manage to eat half a piece of toast. She didn't feel the least bit ready to board a plane in four hours, and she was afraid to be leaving her family for eighteen months.

After borrowing her mom's car to go back home and retrieve

her suitcases, Isabella was ready to go. She helped Rowan and Eliza load up the car. Driving to the airport, Isabella wished they all were going to Italy with her. Tears were forming, and she hadn't even said goodbye yet. Before she knew it, she was standing at the check-in station, where Gloria initiated a group hug.

Isabella broke down in tears and said, "I love y'all so much."

Gloria, Eliza, and Rowan responded in unison, "We love you too."

"Come visit me at Christmas, okay, Momma?" said Isabella.

"You know I'll be there, honey."

Turning to Eliza and Rowan, Isabella added, "And siblings, y'all better visit me too."

They reassured her that they would definitely visit as well.

Then Isabella grabbed her luggage carrier and said, "Okay then. Good. Love y'all." After going through security, she turned around and waved one last time.

As Isabella walked all alone to her seat on the plane, the reality of what had happened that week came rushing in. Isabella knew that her grief would eventually lessen, but right then she just wanted to cry. So she did, all the way across the ocean wide.

Hours later, after the pilot announced the plane would soon be landing, Isabella heard a child praying out loud and thanking God for safe travels. For her, precious words from an innocent child ushered in immeasurable hope. God was enveloping her with a comfort that only He could provide. As she looked out the window toward the runway, her pulse began to race. There it was in big letters—*Italia!*

Grateful for a smooth landing, Isabella was ready to step off the plane and into the next chapter of her life. Eager for a warm bath, she could hardly wait to get to her new home away from home. Back home it was two o'clock in the morning and much too late to call, so Isabella texted her mom that she had arrived and would call later. Hearing people around her speak Italian and other languages felt strange, and Isabella was thankful for her language interpretation pocketbook.

Isabella kept to herself, laser focused on picking up her luggage, but forty-five minutes later there was still no sign of her belongings. "Please, God, don't let me lose the letters. Or the yarn. Please."

"I'll help you look," said a kind voice behind her in English.

Isabella turned around to see a woman with silver hair and caramel skin, probably in her early eighties. Wondering if the woman was traveling alone, she said, "Oh, thank you. I mean, *grazie*. My name is Isabella."

"Nice to meet you, Isabella. My name's Hattie."

Pacing the floor now, Isabella could feel tension building at the thought that her luggage could be lost forever. Sure, the letters were only copies; the originals were safe back home. But she had tied them together with a piece of yarn that her father had given her when she was a little girl, to remind her of God's miraculous power that created the heavens. The yarn's other purpose was to remind her to not lose childlike faith—the same innocent faith that believed in moon strings. On the brink of tears, Isabella tried to take deep breaths.

"What color is your luggage, Miss Isabella?" the woman asked.

"Um, it's a bright blue and white suitcase," replied Isabella, "with something very special inside."

"Well, then, I'm sure God will help us find it."

Isabella was not up for small talk, but she appreciated the kindness. Absolutely beside herself at that point, she couldn't keep from tapping her foot and fidgeting with her hair. With an aching body and red eyes as dry as sandpaper, she was in need of rest.

Twenty minutes later, Hattie was still talking. She had been living in Italy for eight years and working at the bar—in English, a *café*, as Hattie explained—across the street from the local hospital. Hattie and her husband had moved often, from one military base to another, during their thirty-five year marriage. Lawrence passed away twelve years ago. Twice a year Hattie goes back home to visit her mom in New Orleans.

Hearing Hattie, a stranger, talk reminded Isabella of her mom. Already homesick, she teared up.

"Everything all right, dear?" asked Hattie.

"Oh yes, I'm okay. Just missing home."

"Well, here comes some good news for you!" Hattie pointed to a piece of luggage.

Isabella immediately recognized it and exclaimed, "Thank you, Jesus!" With a loud sigh of relief, she reached for her suitcase. "Thanks, Hattie, for staying here with me. Very kind of you."

"You are most welcome. There sure must be something valuable in there," Hattie replied.

"Oh yes, ma'am, there is. Birthday letters from my dad. Well, copies of them."

Hattie said, "Now that's just too wonderful for words. You know, people should start writing letters again. There's just something special about reading a handwritten letter. These days everybody sends texts. Different times, for sure. If you ask me, I'll take a handwritten card or letter instead of a text message any day."

"I know what you mean," responded Isabella. "Me too."

Before they went their separate ways, Hattie asked if Isabella wanted to share any prayer requests. Isabella didn't believe

19

that meeting Hattie had been an accident, so she shared briefly about Brendan and then they both prayed. Sensing God's peace around her, Isabella thanked Hattie for the prayer and bid her farewell.

Once outside the airport, Isabella walked up to the orange sign marked *Taxi* and waited. A few minutes later, she was on her way to the real estate agent's office to pick up the keys to her new home. Filled with wonder, she looked out her window at the Eternal City. The streets were busy with motorcycles, small cars, and tour buses everywhere. Catching a view of the morning sun appearing to weave through billowy clouds, Isabella imagined falling asleep on one of the clouds.

The agent's office was only five minutes from Isabella's new home, where the first thing she noticed was linen curtains waving softly in the gentle breeze through two open windows. Hints of lavender in the air welcomed her, and she was captivated by the appeal of the two-story, tan and white brick double. Potted plants sat on each of the twelve steps leading up to the front doors, and red, pink, and white flowers added the perfect touch. *I wish Mom could see this*, she thought.

Isabella tried several times to call her mom, but the phone kept disconnecting and the calls couldn't go through. Frustrated, she felt her temperature rising, and erratic thoughts came out of nowhere. Fearing that her heart would stop beating and no one would be around to help, Isabella found it difficult to breathe. The more she worried about not being able to breathe, the more difficult it became, and trying to yawn didn't help.

Feeling beat up and aggravated, Isabella walked inside, plopped herself down on the brown leather sofa, and cried loudly. Brendan's death, jet lag, and a new home were enough to set off a full-fledged panic attack. Her arms began shaking out of control, she was overcome with thoughts of a debilitating illness, and then she couldn't stop rubbing her hands together. Gasping for air, she was sure that she was about to suffocate.

Isabella's feelings of shame returned. She had worked so hard to serve God, encourage other people, and read the Bible, and yet these panic attacks were getting stronger. She felt unworthy, unclean. In a world where Christians should have balanced lives, she felt out of place.

An hour or so later, she got up and took a closer look around the apartment, hoping that might make her feel better. Her new home was decorated beautifully with hardwood floors, freshly painted cream walls, and designer furniture right out of a magazine, and her eyes enjoyed taking it all in. With two bedrooms, a bathroom, living room, kitchen, and laundry room, it exceeded Isabella's expectations. She was already imagining how it would look at Christmas. Then it was time for unpacking and a warm bath, and Isabella welcomed the serenity.

Later that night, Isabella grabbed a cup of coffee and went outside to sit on the white linen-covered sofa swing. A cluster of clouds moved swiftly through the star-filled sky, giving the appearance that the moon was sliding down the right-hand side of a cloud. Suddenly two shooting stars dashed across the sky.

"You are mighty, God," she whispered, looking up toward the heavens. "Why did Brendan have to die? Why now? I don't understand." Breaking down in tears, she curled up on the sofa swing. She pictured his smiling face as he held up a croquet mallet, ready to have fun. But then she pictured him in a box and thought about all the things she hadn't said to him while he was alive.

Back inside about an hour later, Isabella finally succeeded in reaching Gloria. "Hey, Momma."

"Sweetie, how are you?" asked her mother. "You sound like you've been crying."

Isabella said, "I'm good. Feels weird that I'm really here. I can't just get in the car and come see you."

"Now sweetheart, hold it together. You need to be okay, Isabella. You've waited your whole life for this moment."

"I know, Momma."

Gloria said, "Hey, no need to raise your voice at me, young lady."

"I'm not, Mom," Isabella insisted.

"Yes, you are."

"I'm just aggravated. I mean, I'm just …" Feeling aggravated about being aggravated, Isabella wanted to start the conversation over. She hadn't wanted to sound argumentative on her first phone call from Italy. Not at all. One of Isabella's internal struggles continued to be about using the right words, and it was happening again.

"Mom, listen, I'm sorry. Please forgive me. I'm really tired, and I'm second guessing whether I made the right decision. My thoughts are all over the place. Just so much going on." Isabella began sobbing.

"Sweetheart, of course I forgive you," Gloria reassured her. "I never know what to say to you, and my words never seem to come out the way I want them to. But please hear this loud and clear—I love you so much, and I'm so proud of you. You are daring to go for your dream, and that's something to be quite proud of, my girl. We're all feeling sad about Brendan. It's okay to cry, honey. God's with you and will hold all your tears."

"I love you, Mom. Thank you."

"I love you, Bella. Now I really want you to get some good rest. Get yourself something to eat and go to bed early. We'll catch up later, and then you can tell me all about the flight and everything, okay?"

"Okay. Good night, Mom. Love you too."

Chapter 3

That night Isabella had the dream about the water and the wolf again, and it left her a bit shaken up. The first line in her journal the next morning was "Are you trying to tell me something, God?"

Isabella's struggle with anxiety has always been real and rough. One minute she would be fine, and the next minute her thoughts would be all over the place. During panic attacks, Isabella feared that her fast-beating heart would surely explode. Her praise to God remains real and her love for Him unwavering, but the relentless fear that she was battling still has no plans of letting go anytime soon.

Until her dad passed away, she had been doing better and experiencing fewer anxious episodes. She was growing in her faith and enjoying being involved with church activities. But when her dad died, the anxiety came back with a vengeance, as did her attempts to hide behind a mask. Afraid of being called a fake Christian because she struggled with anxiety, Isabella began holding in her feelings more. In her opinion, a true Christian wouldn't be subject to fear, so she experienced a lot of guilt.

This was a day for unpacking and relaxing on the sofa swing. Twenty-four hours before Isabella would start to work, her nerves were kicking in. Everyday life back home was routine and comfortable, but here, on the other side of the world, a blank slate had presented itself with new life pages to be written. Oh, how her heart hoped this had been the right decision.

After washing some clothes, Isabella decided to check email and touch base with friends back home. There it was, another email from Vivienne, who had sent three in the past week. Isabella still hadn't responded. Taking a deep breath, she clicked on the most recent message. It was an invitation to join an online Christian Bible study group for people dealing with grief. But Isabella's grief was still too fresh for her to talk about what had happened. Halfway through reading the email, her mind was made up to graciously decline.

An hour later, Isabella turned off the computer and decided to sit outside on the swing. Out there, somehow her sense that God was with her became stronger. God was there, and He was ready for a conversation—ready to listen and encourage. Isabella needed to be heard and encouraged. God was definitely drawing her closer and tugging on her heart in ways that only He could. Picking up her journal and Bible, Isabella headed out the door. Then she began to write about her dream:

Hello, God. So here's my dream. I know that You know what happened. Please help me understand what You want me to know. The dream begins with me standing in an open parking lot by myself. A wolf appears and begins to walk toward me with a look of attack in its eyes. I want to run, but my legs won't move. The wolf stops and gives me a cold stare. Behind the wolf, a small tree sprouts up from the ground. The ground then changes from concrete to grass. Tree roots start to spread underneath. What does this mean, Lord?

Suddenly the wind blew her Bible open to Psalm 51:10. According to the date written in her own handwriting, she had circled this same verse exactly two years ago. Thinking this was not an accident, Isabella prayed the verse out loud: "Create in me a pure heart, O God, and renew a steadfast spirit within me. Do not cast me from your presence or take your Holy Spirit from me. Restore to me the joy of your salvation and grant me a willing spirit, to sustain me."

Ashamed. That's how Isabella felt when she prayed. Burdened by her panic attacks, she hoped God didn't see her dismal faith. All her life she'd found joy in praising God and being in awe of His majestic ways. But she was obsessed with her inability to go back to the past and wipe the slate clean, and she overanalyzed what she should have done in relationships. She wanted to start over, without anxiety:

> *As I stand here, many people stand behind me,*
> *and I notice that we're all wearing armor—helmets,*
> *breastplates, the whole battle gear. Each of us is holding*
> *a shiny sword. Something that looks like a black*
> *rectangle or a brick blocks my vision for a few minutes.*
> *I have no idea what that means! Then doves land on*
> *my shoulder and also on the shoulders of everyone else.*
> *What do You want me to know from this dream? Help*
> *me to hear You, please.*
>
> *Are you trying to tell me something about the*
> *Holy Spirit? Right after the doves land on everyone's*
> *shoulders, we all shout, "Yahweh!" Immediately the*

swords leave our hands and fly toward the wall. Before they reach the wall, the word Yahweh appears on each sword. Then the ground shakes and a gigantic wall begins to crumble. While this is going on, a clear blue river surrounds the wall and drowns the wolf. And that's my dream!

Hands sweating and heart beating fast, Isabella began some deep breathing exercises. The moment was intense, and she could sense a spirit tug from God Himself. Then a dove landed on the front light post, and all Isabella could do was laugh! The rest of the day was quite splendid as she enjoyed baking, reading, and just being. Any time she started to think about Brendan, she tried to distract herself, because it still hurt too much. When night came around, Isabella reflected on the day and felt a strong peace. She slept peacefully the whole night through.

When the elevator door opened, Isabella froze. What an interesting way for her first day of work to begin! Before her stood a man with broad shoulders, lightly gelled black hair, and gorgeous brown eyes with thick eyebrows—a true Italian, for sure. Isabella thought her heart would jump right out of her chest!

"Ciao," said the good-looking man, who was wearing green scrubs.

"Ciao." Isabella brushed her bangs away from her eyes, certain that she was blushing.

"Where are you going?" he asked.

"Well, I'll be here for eighteen months to complete my pulmonology internship, but after that I'm really not sure," Isabella answered, catching her breath. "I might move back to my home in New Orleans, or to Tennessee since I love the mountains. Just have to take it one day at a time."

Clearing his throat, the good-looking man said, "No, I actually meant what floor were you going to?"

Isabella tried her level best to act calm, cool, and collected, but she couldn't hide a nervous giggle. "Fourth floor, please."

"That's where I'm going," the man said. "I need to drop off some X-rays at the front desk. By the way, my name is Lucian."

"I'm Isabella. Nice to meet you, Lucian."

When the elevator doors opened, Lucian went left and Isabella went right. With a quick wave goodbye, she desperately wanted to follow him, but she figured that would be a bit too obvious. In her distraction, she took one wrong turn after another, but twenty minutes later she finally arrived at the clinic's front desk.

"*Buongiorno!* My name is Isabella Cole. I'm the new intern from New Orleans."

"Ciao. I'm Francesca."

Isabella noticed one curler stuck in Francesca's long brown hair. Not wanting to embarrass her new coworker, she mentioned the curler to her.

"Oh, I forgot all about that, and no one else mentioned it. Thank you!" said Francesca.

"You're welcome." Isabella felt like the ice was broken. At least for now, she wasn't feeling too anxious.

Francesca said, "We're so excited that you're here. Later we'll chat and I'll show you around the department, but right now you can shadow me with a few patients, okay?"

"That sounds perfect," agreed Isabella.

"Our first patient should be here any second," said Francesca. "She's sweet, as you'll see."

"I'm here," said a squeaky voice walking up to the front desk. Ten-year-old Giselle was Isabella's first patient.

"Ciao, Giselle. I'm Isabella."

Giselle asked, "Are you going to be my doctor today? I'm wearing my pretty pink dress because it's my birthday." She twirled around slowly, with her oxygen tube in one hand and a sparkly white baton in the other.

"Well, then it's an extra special day!" Isabella declared, making a big circle with both hands as if cheering before an audience. "Yes, I'll be working with Ms. Francesca this morning, so you get to spend time with both of us."

"Good!" exclaimed Giselle, exuding kindness.

Francesca pulled Isabella aside for a moment and explained that four weeks earlier, the doctors had determined that the spot on Giselle's lung was growing rapidly. Eventually the cancer would eat away the lung lining and the cancer would win.

Isabella tried to put on a happy face and not be sad for Giselle. She sensed that the little girl knew what was really going on and was ready to be with Jesus.

Francesca and Isabella took Giselle back to the treatment area, where Francesca said, "We're going to do some tests, okay? Ms. Isabella will be with us."

"Okay, Ms. Francesca," Giselle said, putting down her baton.

As Isabella handed Giselle's chart to Francesca, several loose papers fell to the floor. Feeling clumsy, Isabella apologized for the mess and nervously began picking up the papers.

Then Giselle tapped Isabella's left hand and asked, "Want to know my wish?"

"Why, sure," said Isabella. "What's your birthday wish?"

"I want Mama and Papa to dance again."

"That's a very sweet wish." Isabella wasn't sure what else to say.

Giselle said, "See, they care about me so much. Sometimes I hear them crying in their room, and I know they're talking about me. They don't want me to leave, but I'm ready to go. I know that Jesus loves me. I have Him in my heart, and I'm not afraid to go back home."

Inspired by Giselle's bravery, Isabella was speechless. Smiling as she and Francesca walked with Giselle back to the front desk, Isabella wished she could pray for Giselle. Not sure if that would be allowed, though, she chose to pray silently for the little girl.

At the end of her appointment, Giselle slowly walked down the hall, waving her baton. At each of the four staff offices, she said, "I wish you a happy, God-blessed day! Jesus loves you, and so do I!" With huge smiles, every staff member wished her a happy birthday—and then grabbed a tissue.

When her shift ended, Isabella clocked out and headed toward the parking garage. Her new car had been delivered to the hospital during her shift. Just off the main lobby, however, she noticed the chapel and decided to enter. The open Bible on the podium at the front of the room offered a divine invitation to read. Isabella gently touched the pages, smiled, and walked to the back row, welcoming the silence. Leaning her head against the back wall, she closed her eyes and prayed silently to feel God's peace.

Isabella just wanted the racing thoughts of impending doom to stop. After having such a good day, why was her mind going haywire? She was reminded that sooner or later, she would need to talk about her feelings with someone, but not yet. With a stiff neck, tight shoulders, and sore muscles, Isabella tried to focus. She had to take care of so much other stuff that she didn't think she could bear also being saddled with attending counseling sessions.

After spending several minutes in the quiet chapel, Isabella decided to write in the prayer book: "Please help me, Jesus. I feel like I'm on a roller coaster, and I can't unhook the buckle strapping me in." Then she stared at the page and everything became a bit blurred. Her breathing slowed and she felt faint, so Isabella sat down in the front row—even though she never sat toward the front at church or anywhere else.

Hoping no one else would walk in, Isabella was on edge. Would the new job be a good fit for her? Would she be able to adjust to this new lifestyle? Sure, she had always dreamed of living in Italy, but being there in person was a brand new reality. Isabella was beginning to realize that dreams and reality are two different concepts. Her life was changing, and she was scared.

Isabella had never been afraid of having a panic attack in the middle of a patient's appointment. But now, in this new season, fear had a new playground. Folding her arms around herself as if receiving a hug, Isabella envisioned hugging her family at the airport, and sweet thoughts slowly calmed her down.

Walking out of the main hospital a few minutes later, Isabella didn't happen to see Lucian—but she didn't feel like talking anyway. When she got back home, she ate dinner, put on her pajamas, and climbed into bed. Out of nowhere, feelings of anxiety and depression were building, and her emotions were swirling. Even climbing into bed felt awkward. The bedsheets didn't smell familiar, and the mattress wasn't as soft as back home. Feeling homesick, Isabella cried. She wanted to be happy and felt guilty for being sad. Curled up under the covers, after an hour or so, she finally fell asleep.

Chapter 4

A new day and a blank slate. Anything was possible.

The hospital gift shop had just opened, and Isabella had arrived at work early. So with time to spare, she went in. Decorative scarves and matching purses, coffee mugs, fuzzy blankets, art collections, handmade crosses, inspirational plaques—everything looked quite lovely. Eyeing a beautiful black slanted bookcase that would be perfect for her new home, Isabella walked across the room toward it. Then she noticed Lucian walk in, and they made eye contact. Waving at him with her eyes laser focused on his charming good looks, Isabella tripped on a cord attached to a lamp display.

"*Buongiorno, señora. Come va*?" Lucian stretched out his hand to help Isabella to her feet.

Isabella grabbed his hand, stood up, and dusted off her jeans. "*Grazie*. Wanna hear something funny?"

"Absolutely! Tell me something funny, but first remind me of your name."

Isabella always wove God into every conversation, never knowing whether the person to whom she was talking was a believer. She figured that she could never go wrong bringing the light. That's just who she was, and this was one of those times. "My morning devotional was about God being a lamp unto our feet. Oh, and my name is Isabella."

"Now, that's funny and very cool," said Lucian. "Yeah, God's obvious sometimes, isn't He?"

Encouraged by his response, Isabella replied in kind, "He sure is."

"Hey listen, I have to run. Good to see you, though," said Lucian, handing Isabella a card from his coat pocket.

As he walked out of the gift shop, Isabella looked at the card. It identified Lucian as a guest speaker for an upcoming faith and business seminar at a local church. Deciding quickly, Isabella called after him, "Thanks, I'll be there!" Then she put the card in her purse and headed upstairs to clock in.

"Ciao, Isabella," said Francesca. "Ready for another day?"

Wearing her dark brown hair in a loose side braid, and with just a touch of light purple eye shadow and mascara, Francesca looked refreshed. She hadn't been wearing makeup the previous day, so Isabella wondered if she was going somewhere special. Sometimes Isabella didn't wear eye shadow, powder, or blush, but she couldn't imagine leaving her house without mascara.

"Yes, I'm ready." Isabella raised her right arm as though cheering.

Only Francesca and Isabella were working in the clinic that day. Their three coworkers—two women whom Isabella believed to be in their forties, and a male doctor who was about to retire—were at a conference. Isabella hoped they would enjoy working with her. She hadn't spent much time with them yet, but she hoped to connect with them soon.

Francesca said, "Mr. Antoine is our only patient today. Just so you know, his daughter, Gianna, is having a difficult time since finding out that he has lung cancer. They've been here for about a month, and it's been hard for both of them. So if she seems a bit standoffish, please don't take it personally."

"Thanks for telling me, Francesca," said Isabella. *Focus,*

focus, focus. Jesus, help me do a good job today, she whispered
to herself. Still feeling awkward about dropping the papers on
the previous day, she hoped not to appear clumsy again.

Walking over to greet Gianna, she said, "My name is
Isabella, and I'm new to the clinic. It's nice to meet you."

"Ciao," Gianna replied without looking up from her cell
phone.

"Francesca just took your dad back to the treatment room.
Can I get you anything to drink? A bottled water maybe?"

"No thanks." Gianna remained glued to the phone's screen.

Isabella noticed a tattoo on Gianna's upper left arm with
the numbers 413 inked in blue inside a gold heart. She wanted
to ask about the tattoo, but she decided not to pry. Instead, she
just said, "Hope you have a good day."

"Good?" Gianna snapped at Isabella, looking up from
her phone. "Are you kidding me? How can any part of this
experience be good? It's my twenty-first birthday and I'm here
with my dad. Where's the fun in that? How can seeing my dad
with a tube up his nose be good? How can watching him walk
at a turtle's pace be good? How can …?" Placing both hands
over her face, Gianna began sobbing.

Rarely had Isabella's patients been so open with their
emotions upon first meeting her. Isabella listened for the next
half hour as Gianna opened up the floodgates. No other patients
were expected, so the waiting room was a quiet place just for
them.

Then Gianna unexpectedly told Isabella about her tattoo,
which was designed to remind her that we can do all things
through Christ. She said that Philippians was one of her favorite
books of the Bible, and that people had been telling her not to
be depressed over what was happening with her dad.

Isabella teared up as she listened. She was moved by Gianna's story, but she knew also that the Holy Spirit was speaking to Gianna. By the end of their visit, Gianna told Isabella that she felt much lighter. Gianna's heart had been hardened, and letting someone in, especially a stranger, had been the furthest thing from her mind that morning. But Isabella was welcomed into Gianna's heart by the grace of God.

The rest of Isabella's morning was spent reviewing policies and procedures. With the clinic open only half a day, she had time to spare. She tried calling Gloria, Eliza, and Annalise, but got no answer. Feeling far from home, Isabella was lonely. Not sure what to do with the rest of her day, she decided to take a tour of the city, so she got a taxi and headed for the Trevi Fountain.

According to tradition, based on books that Isabella had read about Italy, anyone who throws coins in the fountain will someday find themselves in Rome again. Isabella was ready to make a splash, so she reached into her purse for three coins. She had dreamed of that moment for years! Holding the coins in her right hand with her back to the fountain, Isabella shouted, "To returning here, to a new romance, and to marriage one day!" Then she threw the coins over her left shoulder and into the fountain. It was a moment that Isabella would remember forever.

People were everywhere, snapping photos or simply sitting down to enjoy their lunch. One bride-to-be was posing for wedding photos in front of the fountain. Isabella watched with joy as the photographer set the scene, and she pictured her own wedding day. The little girl inside, who had dreamed of someday being in that very place, was witnessing that dream coming true. Sitting on the fountain's edge for a few minutes, Isabella whispered, "Thanks, God, for all this. I love you."

Noticing three designer clothing shops—Dolce and

Gabbana, Gucci, and Versace—Isabella decided to have fun trying on clothes. In the dressing room trying on her third dress, she felt a bit lightheaded but tried not to pay it any attention.

A bit later, with a bag full of three blouses, Isabella walked to a nearby *ristorante*. Francesca and Hattie happened to be there, and they were excited to see her walk in. Isabella was delighted to see them too. A girls' day in Italy! They enjoyed cappuccino and showing their recent purchases to one another. After visiting for an hour or so, Hattie drove Francesca and Isabella back to their homes. It had been a good day, and Isabella was quite tired.

Before going to sleep, Isabella picked up her journal. Some grand and rather fantastic moments recorded in those pages made her heart quite thankful when she went back to read them. It was the other entries, however, that challenged her. That stronghold, the one Isabella wouldn't talk about with anyone, had a grip that was getting tighter. Every time Isabella read the journal pages written in mid-panic mode, she wept. Deep inside, she felt responsible for the choices made by other people that had led them down unfortunate paths. As she replayed conversations, over and over in her mind, in which she had tried to offer hope, Isabella wondered if she had spoken wisely.

Just as her eyes were closing, a text came through from her mom: "I was reading Psalm 91 right now and felt led to encourage you to read it. Have a blessed evening."

Isabella texted back to thank her mom, and then began reading:

> He who dwells in the shelter of the Most High
> will rest in the shadow of the Almighty. I will
> say of the Lord, He is my refuge and my fortress,

> my God in whom I trust. Surely he will save
> you from the fowler's snare and from the deadly
> pestilence. He will cover you with his feathers,
> and under his wings you will find refuge; his
> faithfulness will be your shield and rampart.
> (Psalm 91:1-4)

Isabella placed the phone down, closed her eyes, and began to pray. "Lord, I know you are with me. I know that because the Bible tells me so, and every word in there is true. I feel like I'm letting you down, like I'm a hypocrite. I know your feathers and your wings shield me. I know that was true when I was a little girl talking to you about moon strings. But I'm starting to have more panic attacks. Why can't I make the attacks stop? Sometimes I feel numb and lost, like I'm about to fall apart. Is something wrong with me?"

Squeezing her pillow tight, Isabella lay still. After five minutes or so had passed, she picked up her phone to finish reading the prayer:

> You will not fear the terror of night, nor the
> arrow that flies by day, nor the pestilence that
> stalks in the darkness, nor the plague that
> destroys at midday. A thousand may fall at your
> side, ten thousand at your right hand, but it will
> not come near you. You will only observe with
> your eyes and see the punishment of the wicked.
> If you make the Most High your dwelling—even
> the Lord, who is my refuge—then no harm will
> befall you, no disaster will come near your tent.
> For he will command his angels concerning you
> to guard you in all your ways; they will lift you

up in their hands, so that you will not strike
your foot against a stone. (Psalm 91:5-12)

Isabella stopped reading, put down the phone, and covered
her face with both hands. "God, I know you're here. Is this
about my dream? Is this about me seeing that wolf staring at
me as though it wants to rip me to shreds? Are you trying to
tell me something with the psalm?"

Then she envisioned heavenly angels surrounding her—
standing behind, beside, and in front as the wolf looked on.
"Is this dream actually a vision with a purpose that I don't
understand yet? Are you giving me visions like you gave Joseph
that he needed to pay attention to? I really need you to protect
my thoughts. I just want to be used by you and let the world
know how amazing you are, but I'm not sure if I'm doing a
good job with that. Can you still use me for good, even though I
suffer with those mental barrages of fear? Please help me, Jesus."

You will tread upon the lion and the cobra;
you will trample the great lion and the serpent.
'Because He loves me,' says the Lord, 'I will rescue
him; I will protect him, for he acknowledges my
name. He will call upon me, and I will answer
him; I will be with him in trouble, I will deliver
him and honor him. With long life will I satisfy
him and show him my salvation.' (Psalm 91:13-16)

With both arms raised, Isabella loudly declared the prayer's
promise: "For he will command his angels concerning you to
guard you in all your ways. Please help me sleep peacefully
tonight, Jesus. I love you." Isabella held the open journal to her
cheek as if giving the Lord above a hug.

She had a peaceful sleep.

Chapter 5

"*Buongiorno,* Francesca. *Come va?*" Hoping none of her coworkers would detect her anxiety, Isabella tried to appear calm.

Francesca looked up with bloodshot eyes and said, "Ciao."

"Feeling okay?" Isabella knew just by looking at Francesca that she wasn't feeling good at all. "Can I get you a tea from the café?"

"No. Thanks, though," said Francesca. "I'm eating crackers. My stomach's all messed up. I thought about calling in sick. I don't know if I'm coming down with something. I wiped down all the phones and keyboards just in case."

Isabella said, "If you need anything, let me know."

"Okay, I will," agreed Francesca. Then she stood up and added, "I'll be back in just a minute."

Walking toward the waiting room, Isabella looked back and said, "Okay. I really hope you feel better."

Francesca simply nodded in reply.

Twenty minutes later, Francesca still hadn't returned. Isabella was busy reviewing charts in her office. Getting up to go to the restroom, she saw Francesca hunched over in the hallway.

"Is everything all right?" asked Isabella. "Anything I can do?"

"Can you turn back the clock and erase what happened?" Francesca responded. "I don't think so ... I'm sorry, Isabella. I didn't mean to snap at you. I'm just freaking out right now."

Isabella told Francesca that she was going downstairs for tea. Fifteen minutes later, the two women sat in Isabella's office with hot tea in hand.

Fidgety, Francesca began to share. "One night I decided to cook dinner for him. We had been dating only about two months. Well, one thing led to another, and you can figure out the rest. The next day, he told me things were moving too fast—but that hadn't mattered to him when I slept over!"

Isabella said, "I don't have the perfect words, Francesca, but I will pray for you. Just remember, there's nothing you have done or will ever do that can take away God's love for you. His mercy and grace are always there for you." Isabella's words were speaking to her own heart.

"Mercy and grace? Are you kidding me?" replied Francesca. "I'm beyond mercy and grace. I sure didn't receive grace in the moment to stop me from making a stupid mistake. Why didn't God keep this from happening to me? Where was He?" She began sobbing. "I must sound like a fool. You probably haven't had a bad day in your life. You seem so happy."

"Listen to me, Francesca," said Isabella. "I'm not perfect, not at all. Believe me. And my life has not always been easy. Honestly, I'm going through some things right now." Then she caught herself, not wanting to share details.

Francesca said, "I know you mean well. It's just that if I walked into church right now, the building would probably go up in flames. Listen, I just need some fresh air. I'll be back in a little bit."

Isabella offered a nod of understanding and then began praying silently for Francesca to be at peace.

Shortly thereafter, Francesca walked back into the clinic and said, "I'm back, Isabella."

Suddenly Isabella noticed a lizard on Francesca's shoe and dashed across the room at warp speed. "There's a lizard on your shoe. They freak me out!"

Looking down at her shoe, Francesca shrieked, "Ah, it came in from outside!"

Everyone laughed as Francesca feverishly swirled around, trying to rid her shoe of the lizard. Isabella could barely contain herself. When the lizard leaped off Francesca's shoe and onto the computer, where it looked directly at her, she screamed—but her tears had been replaced with laughter. A couple of minutes later, the lizard leaped off the computer, ran across the floor, and scurried out the door. Nobody could catch it—or stop looking at their own shoes.

Right before time to head home, Francesca found the courage to call her doctor's office and make an appointment.

Isabella was proud of her new friend, and she prayed for Francesca all the way home. Her heart felt light. She had enjoyed laughing and listening to someone share their own struggle. God had used her in a special way, to light the way for a weary soul, and Isabella was at peace.

Chapter 6

Isabella awoke to a ringing phone.

It was Annalise. "Hey, Isabella. How are you, my friend? So sorry I haven't called. Steven and I took the kids on a ministry retreat this week."

"Hey, my friend! I'm okay. Just waking up and about to start my day," said Isabella.

"We've been missing Brendan a lot," Annalise said. "The kids loved him so much."

Certain that Annalise was going to keep asking how she was doing, Isabella was already rehearsing a positive reply. She was too embarrassed to mention her anxiety.

A few years ago, Isabella had volunteered at a Christmas ladies' event at church. Her job had been to stand at the entrance, smile at the attendees, and hand out programs. After about fifteen minutes, she had begun feeling dizzy. Immediately she had felt like all eyes were on her and the walls were closing in. The more she had desperately tried to catch her breath and calm down, the worse she had felt. Isabella had run straight to the restroom just as Annalise happened to be walking out. When Isabella had broken down in tears, Annalise had assured her that everything would be okay. Isabella had shared with Annalise a bit about feeling anxious, but she hadn't gone into detail despite Annalise's questions.

Isabella had felt like a fake Christian back then, because of her battle with fear, and she felt the same way now. So she wasn't ready to talk about what was going on inside, at least not yet.

Annalise said, "You sound good, Isabella. We're praying for you to do great, and we all want to visit soon. Well, I have to run, but I want to remind you that the Lord is for you and you've got nothing to fear. Be encouraged."

"I'm praying for you too, friend. Y'all take care. Thanks so much for calling," said Isabella.

After hanging up, Isabella made a cup of coffee and sat down to check email. "Read this" was the subject of an email that Gloria apparently had sent Isabella the previous night. Attached was an article that Isabella had written some years ago for a women's retreat at church, back when she had felt a little better about herself. Gloria mentioned in the email that she had come across the article while she was clearing out her inbox.

Isabella didn't believe that her mom had *accidentally* come across the email, so she began reading:

Perspective. The other day I was reminded that each day presents new opportunities to have a first-row seat to watch God move in the lives of those around me. When patients enter the doctor's office where I work, I never know what to expect. I don't know if they are having a good day or one of their worst days ever. Some arrive happy and some burst into tears. But this I do know, that I can never go wrong by building up others with genuine words of encouragement. A few words spoken kindly multiply into volumes of hope to a heart that is searching for a listening ear, especially when someone is in pain. *Listening, actively listening, is a lost art that needs to resurface.*

Isabella stopped reading, and a chill came over her. Staring at the floor, she broke down upon realizing that *she* was the one who needed encouragement. Then she continued reading:

Is there someone in your life who needs encouragement? Do you? Truth be told, everyone is either in a struggle, has just emerged from a battle, or is about to enter a trial. Perhaps some of you can relate to what I'm saying. Never be ashamed of anything that has happened to you in the past. God is sovereign, and nothing takes Him by surprise. Although He is not the author of our pain, He is always in control of what He allows to happen in our lives. We cannot begin to imagine why certain things happen, because His ways are much higher than ours. However, we can place our trust in Him and dare to believe that He will, in His own time, reveal the purpose of our pain. As a result, we will be on the road to healing, and in turn, be able to sincerely offer encouragement to other people who are struggling.

Don't be fooled. You never know who's fighting a battle. Someone might look happy on the outside despite the fact that a hurricane is roaring inside. This is one reason why I remain mindful and never assume anything about a patient who walks into the clinic. I remain professional, seeking to provide them with the

*best possible care, and I shine my light in their direction
and hope that they see God's reflection. Be encouraged
that there is hope as you place your trust in God. When
we put our trust in Him, healing has permission to
enter and take up residence.*

*I encourage you to never hold back from sharing
your testimony of how God has moved in your life. You
might wonder if you even have a testimony to share,
but I promise that you do. If you have ever struggled
with despair, anxiety, fear, depression, grief, and the list
goes on, you have a unique opportunity. God will show
you His purpose in the pain. Let your light shine to
everyone whom He places around you, and never forget
that you have purpose.*

The words moved Isabella's soul. Once again, God's timing
was perfect. She remembered writing that article, as well as
the anxiety attack that had happened when she had walked
into the grocery store that night. Waiting in a long checkout
line, Isabella had felt like she was about to pass out, but she had
never told anyone. What would they say to someone who said
they had faith but continued to struggle in that area? That was
her fear still. A part of her still wanted to "save face" in front of
other people, especially when she walked into church.

Looking at her watch, Isabella realized that the faith and
business seminar was starting in an hour. It was her day off,
so she would be able to attend both sessions. Turning off her
computer, she made a peanut butter and banana sandwich to
enjoy as she sat by the living room window. Opening the blinds,
she smelled the scent of lavender. She looked down the street

and watched an elderly couple strolling along, holding hands. Her mind wandered, and her heart dreamed of the day she would hold her true love's hand. Then, realizing it would take at least a half hour to get to the seminar, Isabella hurried to get ready.

By Isabella's observation, at least three hundred people were in the church when she arrived. She was delightfully surprised when Lucian walked up to the podium with microphone in hand. "Hello. My name is Lucian Giordano. First things first, I want to thank the local churches, community leaders, and hospital staff for coordinating today's Strategic Faith Conference. Will you join me in giving them all a round of applause?" The audience began clapping. Isabella, excited as could be, was sure she clapped the loudest and the longest.

Noticing her seated in the center of the third row, Lucian winked. With blushing cheeks, Isabella smiled in return. Isabella usually chose the back row when attending church or seminars. That way, if a panic attack started mounting, she could easily escape the four walls. But today she was trying to put on a brave face, hoping that fear wouldn't win.

Lucian adjusted his reading glasses, sipped some water, and then took a deep breath. "I've been with the hospital for eight years, working as a cardiac nurse. My hope is that through sharing strategic ways in which I apply biblical principles to my daily life, you all will leave here inspired and with a renewed sense of purpose. Please follow along with me by referring to the conference handout sheet you received at the registration desk. It will serve as a great resource for personal study." Isabella, eager as could be, placed the handout sheet on top of her leather binder.

"'Therefore everyone who hears these words of mine and puts them into practice is like a wise man who built his house on the rock.' Jesus spoke these words a long time ago, and the principle remains applicable today." All of a sudden Lucian's microphone went out. He tapped it twice, but there was no sound. Although he tapped it again, there was still no sound. Stepping away from the podium, Lucian walked swiftly to the sound booth. A couple of minutes passed while someone went to look for a new microphone. Then Lucian started coughing persistently.

Isabella remembered putting two strawberry lozenges in her purse that morning. Quickly getting up from her seat, she walked toward Lucian. "Here you go. I thought you might like a lozenge or two."

Taking the lozenges out of her purse and nearly dropping them, Isabella giggled nervously. Then she placed both in his hand.

"Now, that's sweet," Lucian said. "Thank you, Isabella. I don't know what happened. Maybe the water went down the wrong way. Pray for me up there, all right?" Lucian lifted his right hand, inviting her to give him a high-five.

"Will do." Isabella went to give him a high-five and missed. She not only laughed, but snorted. Their second attempt at a high-five was a success. "I'm already loving your presentation. You look great. I mean, it sounds great!" Isabella giggled nervously again. "Better get back to my seat. Have fun up there!" Lucian grinned. Isabella, feeling like she might faint from his charm, fanned herself with the handout sheet when she sat back down.

Now with a different microphone, Lucian stepped up to the podium. The audience began clapping for him. Once again, Isabella was quite certain she clapped the loudest and the longest. How her heart was hoping he'd notice.

"No organization, regardless of the service it provides or the product it sells, is immune to external influences," Lucian said. "It must be prepared not only for success but also for factors that can have negative effects. The same is true for us. In our pursuit of success, we must be careful not to become prideful, whether it be related to our spiritual life or our profession. We also must be prepared for change to come without warning. What happens to your faith when the unexpected happens? When your world is shaken, do you shake too?"

Those words he just spoke are meant for me, aren't they, God? An inner assurance that she was in the conference room by divine providence filled Isabella's soul. *I know you have me here for a reason. Speak to me, Lord.* Then she smiled as if sending the smile straight to God Himself.

"We must remember that temporary trials and frustrations are just that," Lucian continued. "Temporary. Please note that in no way am I minimizing how difficult and challenging life issues can be. Instead my intent is to empower and encourage. Take a look with me now at the scripture verse Isaiah 40:31 printed on your handout. Please read it aloud with me."

Isabella cleared her throat and began to read along. "Yet those who wait for the Lord will gain new strength; they will mount up with wings like eagles, they will run and not get tired, they will walk and not become weary." *Help me rise on eagle's wings, Lord.* A flashback moment then came vividly to mind of Christmas Day four years earlier. It was on that day when Isabella had given her father a small gold sailboat atop a marble stand. The very same scripture verse was inscribed on it with an eagle in flight drawn above. *I miss you, Daddy. I miss you so much. I'm not going to give up, I promise.* Isabella sniffled and then refocused on listening to Lucian.

"I must identify my weaknesses and find ways to grow," Lucian said. "Admittedly in the past I have struggled with doubt, impatience, and pride. I often tried to convince God that I knew how my prayers should be answered. Puffed up with pride—that was me, until the day He broke me. My wife, Sophia, was six months pregnant when a brain aneurysm took her and our unborn baby out of this world and through the gates of heaven. She had become very sick two months earlier with diabetes and blood clots. I kept trying to convince God that He needed to heal Sophia." Lucian paused. Isabella's eyes welled up with tears. Never had she thought that Lucian would have such a story. Her heart filled with compassion. The room was silent.

Adjusting his reading glasses, Lucian looked out toward the auditorium with a nod. In that moment, Isabella thought he was the most beautiful man she'd ever laid eyes on. His beauty was certainly on the outside, but what was inside shone through his tanned skin with an angelic glow. Yes, in him, she could see and feel God more clearly than ever before.

"God wanted my dependence, my heart, my trust," he continued. "Even with my quickness to make my own demands, the creator of the universe never wavered in His love for me. Some say my faith is a crutch. Let me be clear and set the record straight. Faith is not my crutch. Faith is my sword. To anyone here today who thinks it is weak to admit you read the Bible, let me encourage you to read about the victorious battles King David experienced. Go find out about the courage of Joshua, a mighty man of God."

Nudging the woman seated to her right, Isabella whispered, "He's such a great speaker, isn't he?"

The woman smiled and winked. "Yes. He's my grandson." Isabella, surprised at the coincidence, smiled back.

During the next hour, Lucian focused on sharing more of his personal strategic plan, which was built to increase his faith based on business models that examine strengths, weaknesses, opportunities, and threats. "I want to let you all know that if you've ever felt like no one would understand what you're going through, there is hope. You and I may not have the same life experiences, but one thing is true: I can relate to pain. My desire is for others to be drawn to the Lord through my testimony. I'm not perfect. But I do seek after the One who is flawless.

"Search the Holy Scriptures. You will never be the same. Allow Him to enter your life and begin to do transforming work. He will show you there is purpose in your pain. He will replace your sorrow with joy. In turn, He will use you to encourage others on their journey toward healing. It is not by chance that we are all in this room today. Whatever God sets in motion is a divine appointment. Before we conclude, I have a final thought to share." Lucian reached into his coat pocket and pulled out one cent. "'Are not two sparrows sold for a penny? Yet not one of them will fall to the ground apart from the will of Your Father. And even the very hairs of your head are all numbered. So don't be afraid; you are worth more than many sparrows.' Remember, you have a God-given purpose. Be encouraged and go change this world for Him."

Isabella turned toward her now familiar neighbor in the lecture hall. "What a speech! Gave me goose bumps! He sounds like a pastor. Such a great heart."

After Lucian's speech ended with a standing ovation, Isabella decided to walk toward him and extend congratulations on a job well done. Trying to do a bit of a hair flip with her hand did not go as expected. Isabella caught her watch on a long necklace she was wearing. To make matters worse, the necklace got wrapped around her shirt button. Standing now in front of Lucian looking quite awkward, Isabella burst with belly laughter and a snort.

Lucian started to laugh too. "I'm not laughing at you, I promise!" Seconds later her watch clasp came unhooked and untangled from the necklace. Lucian saw Isabella's watch fall and caught it in midair. "Guess you could say I've got some time on my hands!" Lucian and Isabella exchanged phone numbers and planned to meet for lunch at the Spanish Steps the following weekend. There it was in black ink, right before her eyes: Lucian's phone number. Wondering if this could be the beginning of something special, Isabella was already fantasizing about their first date. After the seminar was over, she headed home with an uplifted spirit.

Right before heading to bed, Isabella called her mom, who answered on the first ring.

"*Buongiorno*, Isabella! *Come va?*"

"*Buongiorno*, Momma!"

"Wonderful to hear your voice, sweetheart. How are you?"

"Wonderful to hear your voice too, Momma. How's everything?"

"Going well, honey." Gloria was trying to stay upbeat for Isabella. "I have to tell you, this morning two butterflies were flying around me the entire time I was on the deck. They were beautiful."

"That's so sweet, Momma. Remember when a butterfly landed on my finger? I wish I could find that picture."

"I do remember. We printed copies of that picture, I know it. I'll look through the photo albums later and see if I can find it. Oh, and by the way, I'm going to the doctor next week to find out about my knees. They've been hurting a lot. But don't you worry. I'll be fine."

"What day is your appointment?"

"Next Wednesday. Pray it all goes well, okay?"

"I will, Momma. Hey, do you think you'll be able to come here at Christmas?"

"Absolutely! That's another reason I'm trying to get my knees checked out. I want to feel good so you and I can go touring all around Italy. Really looking forward to that, sweetheart."

Isabella's tone became somber. "Same here, Momma."

"Sweetheart, is everything all right? You sound upset."

"I'm okay. Just tired. I do have something kind of fun to share."

"Oh really? And what would that be?"

Gloria and Isabella spoke for another hour about the seminar, Lucian, and her work. At times during the call Isabella would close her eyes and pretend she was back at Gloria's house, sitting on the sofa visiting. The images of sharing coffee with her mom and reminiscing warmed her soul. Oh, how thankful she was that her mom was just a phone call away.

Later that night Isabella opened her bedroom window to let in fresh air. A soft breeze moved through the sheers. She turned on her computer to listen to LifeSongs. Soon she felt like she was back at home. That was a good feeling. A calm feeling. A healing feeling. Isabella put on her pajamas and was about to climb into bed for a good night's rest. Within three minutes of placing her head on the pillow, she had a strong prompting to read the story of Joseph. *I'll read it in the morning. I'm too sleepy right now*, she thought. But the prompting only grew stronger.

Isabella carried a cup of hot tea and a pen to the front room. After climbing into the sofa chair, comfortable as could be, she began reading. Joseph's story of visions, forgiveness, perseverance, and favor touched her soul once again. The story came alive as if it was the very first time she had ever read about him. Isabella clutched the Bible tightly, wondering what her own dreams meant. "What is the purpose of the wolf? Please tell me, Lord," she whispered.

In her dream that night, Isabella saw herself asking and praying to know the wolf's significance. Then her subconscious envisioned words written on notebook pages: *The wolf represents fear and faith. If you don't take a step, the wolf will grow stronger. It will prevail over you. It can smell fear. Don't let your guard down.* Isabella awoke suddenly in a sweat.

After lying still for about ten minutes, stunned by the dream, she went back into a dream state to find more words appearing in the notebook: *If you do step forward, the wolf will lunge for you, seeking to devour you, but it will fail. Adhere to wise counsel. Seek the Lord. Do not let regret eat away at your flesh. Do not grow angry in the waiting. Do not condemn yourself. Pick up the mighty sword of faith and exchange your weakness for God's strength. Learn from the past but don't let it define you. Lead others to glory's path.*

An hour later—and in awe—Isabella fell fast asleep.

Chapter 7

An *hour early.* For some unknown reason, those three words had echoed in Isabella's mind the previous night—all night long, as a matter of fact. She had woken up sweating at one o'clock, two thirty, and three forty-five. Each time Isabella felt the urge to pray.

Today's four-hour shift was supposed to involve reviewing charts and returning phone calls. Isabella was ready for a peaceful day. The only sound was from LifeSongs streaming through her phone—a good feeling. So far there was nothing out of the ordinary to reveal a possible connection with the whole hour-early thought. That is, until Gianna walked in.

Gianna walked up to the front desk where Isabella was seated. Wearing a black fitted blouse, jeans, and flats, Gianna seemed to Isabella to be a fashionista. But sensing this was not the time to discuss clothes, Isabella didn't mention it. "Ciao, Gianna. Good to see you. Everything all right?" Isabella double-checked the computer to make sure they hadn't accidentally scheduled any appointments today. There were none.

"I'm on my way to a doctor's appointment on the fifth floor," Gianna said. "I'm an hour early." She began fumbling with her keys. "You're from New Orleans, right?"

With no clue about why Gianna was asking, Isabella answered, "Yep, born and raised."

Gianna was still looking at her keys. "Um. Well. Recently, a friend of mine passed away. I knew him from when I was an exchange student in New Orleans three years ago. He was friends with the family I stayed with. Maybe you knew him." With eyes still focused on the keys, Gianna kept fumbling.

Isabella got a sinking feeling. There was no way that her patient's daughter could possibly be speaking about Brendan. No way. That would just be impossible. "What was his name?"

"Brendan," Gianna whispered.

"He was my friend." Isabella teared up. "Such a bright light for Jesus. I miss him."

Gianna looked pale. "I have to go. Can we, maybe, have lunch next door today? I need to talk."

"Sure, Gianna. Meet you there at eleven forty-five."

"Okay, thanks." Gianna walked out the door.

Isabella was once again in a quiet office. Thoughts of Brendan raced through her mind. So did guilt. So did flashbacks of the number of times she'd had to say goodbye too soon. During the next few hours, Isabella felt depressed and tired. Nervous energy began to take over as she contemplated what Gianna might say.

Finishing her shift, Isabella locked the office and headed out to meet Gianna. Arriving on time for lunch, they walked in together. Only a few patrons were there, so the room was quiet and calm. Isabella took in the smells of baked bread and coffee, only to be reminded that somehow it smelled just like back home.

"Thanks for being here, Isabella. I need to talk."

"No problem. Let's go place our order first, okay?" Isabella and Gianna walked up to the counter. They each ordered mozzarella-and-tomato flatbread sandwiches with raspberry tea. Isabella believed it was no accident that the Lord had placed a hurting heart in front of her and that the hurting heart could relate to her own pain.

"Well, how you do you like that! Two of my favorite people. In my bar!"

"So good to see you, Hattie," said Isabella, who knew the day's lunch meeting was no accident. God knew the three women needed to be together, and they were about to find out why.

"Ciao, Mrs. Hattie." Gianna hugged Hattie tightly. "Miss you. I know it's been six months since I've been at church. I'll come back soon."

"That will be a good day, Gianna. We all love you. Isabella, you can come to church too."

Right then Gianna opened up. Right then Isabella closed up. "We both knew Brendan," Gianna told Hattie. "I included him in a group text about a mission trip around the time of his accident. What if I caused him to die?" She broke down in tears.

With hands shaking and every breath becoming a struggle, Isabella found herself right in the middle of a flight-or-fight moment. Escaping to the restroom, she went into a stall and wept. Five minutes later Isabella walked back up to the table.

"Sorry, guys. It's just…" Bowing her head, Isabella didn't know what else to say.

"It's all right, Bella. It's all right." Hattie patted Isabella's folded hands.

"Listen, I have to go check on my dad," Gianna said. "Maybe we can have lunch next week?"

"Of course we can. I'll call you," said Isabella. The look of desperation in Gianna's eyes signaled to Isabella that pain was there. Isabella knew the three of them would need to have more lunch meetings—meetings to lift up and encourage. Isabella didn't know who needed encouraging the most.

Bidding farewell to Gianna and Hattie, Isabella walked back toward the garage. On the way she kept repeating to herself, "Everything will be okay. I know you're with me, God. Everything will be okay."

As Isabella exited the hospital garage and pulled out into the street after looking left and right, she noticed an oncoming car. Certain the other driver would stop at the traffic light, Isabella didn't think danger was imminent. But when the car sped through the light, Isabella feared the worst. Sounds of screeching brakes haunted her ears. Gripping the wheel, she tensed every inch of her body. As she felt shards of glass cutting her face while being violently thrust forward, Isabella screamed on the inside, *No! No! No! Please, God! No!*

As if looking at the crash scenario from up above, Isabella saw the accident take place in slow motion in her mind's eye. She saw herself fly through the windshield, shattering glass. But she saw something else too. As the movie played in her mind, she saw something grand: large white feathers surrounded the car, and a cross and a heart appeared in the center.

"Twenty-eight-year-old. Driving from the hospital. Bring her to trauma now!"

"Who? Bring who to trauma? Who? Wait, what's going on! Can anyone hear me? Why can't anyone answer me? Help me, Jesus!"

The words about bringing a twenty-eight-year-old to trauma echoed twice more in her mind and then faded away. Isabella was not alone, and somehow she knew it. Even as this tragic episode was developing, she knew the Holy Spirit and the hosts of heaven were with her. Just as curtains move to each side of a stage, revealing the image to the audience, so did the heavens seem to open. A valley appeared before her, surrounded by ominous-looking mountains. The valley, dark and with no visible life present, appeared cold. Suddenly a beam of light shone from the sky down into the center of the earth, illuminating the center of the valley. A circle of light with flashes of gold began orbiting the beam. Nothing was holding it from above. Nothing was supporting it from beneath.

Words then appeared within the circle. *Hold fast in your heart my truth that I ordained the apostle Matthew to write about light. These truths are for you, Isabella. My word says you are the light of the world. You, my precious daughter, are like a city set on a hill that cannot be hidden. You cannot be hidden from my plans for you.*

In her heart Isabella spoke out to the God she loved. *"I love you, Father. Please protect me. Am I dying?"* Just then more words appeared in the circle surrounding the light. *Isabella, my child, I have placed you in the world for such a time as this to bring salvation to the ends of the earth.*

The circle slowly began to turn red, eventually encompassing the entire circle and beam. Marvelous light illuminated the valley as Isabella saw what appeared to be her right hand holding a sword with a cross carved deep within. Isabella did not see or hear anything else as the vision disappeared, leaving her heart in wonder.

Chapter 8

A tear fell down Isabella's cheek. *God? What's going on? Why can't I open my eyes? God? God?* Isabella was moving in and out of consciousness.

"Isabella, I'm Dr. Impastato. I believe in the power of prayer and that miracles happen every day. Miracles have happened here. I am praying for a miracle for you today."

I can hear you! Dr. Impastato, I can hear you! Can you hear me? Please call my mom. Please! She could hear the sound of shoes shuffling. Isabella hoped they belonged to Lucian.

"How is she, Dr. Impastato?" Isabella recognized Lucian's voice instantly.

I can hear you, Lucian! I can hear both of you! Can you hear me? Please call my momma.

"It's serious, Lucian. Isabella suffered an acute subdural hematoma. Her pupils remain dilated, and she is unresponsive to touch."

Isabella could hear bits and pieces of the conversation between Lucian and Dr. Impastato. *Look, can y'all see my arms moving? I'm trying! Is it working?*

"Dr. Impastato, would you mind praying with me for Isabella?"

"Absolutely, Lucian. Absolutely. May God give you all comfort and restore you to perfect health. May He infuse you with healing only He can provide. May God and His angels protect you, Isabella. In Jesus's name. Amen."

"Amen. Thank you, Dr. Impastato."

"You're welcome, Lucian. I have to be on my way. You take care."

I heard the prayer! Is my hand moving yet? I'm trying.

"Isabella, can you hear me?"

I can! I can hear you, Lucian! I can hear you! Please get me home! I'm ready to go home. Why can't they hear me, Lord? Please tell them I'm awake.

"I wish you could hear me. I spoke to your mom. We're all praying for you—your mom, your whole family. You've got an army storming the heavens on your behalf. They are planning to come here soon. Your mom told me that you brought copies of birthday letters that your dad wrote you. She told me you had them on a dresser in your new home. Since the hospital gave me your keys, I went by there two days ago and picked up a letter to read to you."

Two days ago? Wait a second. Weren't you just in here praying with Dr. Impastato? That wasn't two days ago. That was two minutes ago. Right? Isabella had in fact lost two days. Aching inside, she wished both her parents were there. The little girl inside was frightened and holding on with every ounce of strength she had.

"Happy birthday, Princess. Do you realize that we have now said 'Happy birthday, Princess' sixteen times? Wow. Sixteen times. That's a lot!"

Hearing Lucian read her father's written words to her, Isabella broke down inside. Her heart cried out in desperation, wishing she was back in the comfort of home, surrounded by her family and friends, celebrating with letter in hand.

*"We have also said, 'Good morning, Isabella' about
5,840 times. We have said, 'Go to bed, turn off the
television, lower the stereo, and do your homework'
an unbelievable number of times. We have said, 'Good
night, Isabella' about 5,840 times, and of course, we
have said, 'I love you' a lot of times. Or have we? Really,
how many times have we told you that we love you?
Probably fewer times than we think. Parents take many
things for granted, Isabella—many things that we just
presume. For example, we naturally presume that you
brush your teeth every night, though we don't check.
We presume that you do your homework on time,
though we don't stare at you in your room for two hours
every night. We presume that you pick good friends,
though we don't demand that we meet each one of
them. We presume that you are happy, though we don't
psychoanalyze you every day."*

Isabella pictured herself as a teen, slamming her bedroom
door after arguing with her parents. Oh, how she wished she
could take back those moments of disrespect. *Please, God, please
let Mom and Dad know I'm sorry for the way I disrespected them.
I didn't mean to slam the door when they were just trying to love
me. Can you forgive me?* It was as if Isabella was right back into
being a teenager. All the emotions of that time came flooding
back with every word Lucian read. The words spoke to her then,
and they were speaking to her heart now.

*"We presume that you know we love you, though
we don't always show it in a way that is easily*

*understandable. Showing love, sometimes, is very
difficult, complicated, and involved. Sometimes it's
painful for the recipient, like being grounded for two
weeks. Presumption, on the part of a parent, can be a
compliment, or it can be a terrible mistake. It can be a
compliment in that we feel that you are close enough to
us to know our feelings and motives. It can be a terrible
mistake in that you may have misinterpreted some
action of ours as being unloving.*

*"I guess what I'm trying to say, Isabella, is really
two things. I want you to know, beyond a doubt,
that we—your mother and I, Rowan, Eliza, and
Grandma—really do love you. As a matter of fact, you
will probably never know just how much we do. We
will never stop loving you. The second thing has to do
with the little picture at the top of this page. I cut the
picture out of the newspaper last week and saved it for
this letter. When I saw the picture, I thought of your
sixteenth birthday. There's a common factor between
the two. The picture portrays the ducklings leaving the
nest. In the picture, the nest is the hatching place for the
ducks."*

In that moment, Isabella's heart hoped her words would
reach the heavens. *Dad, can you hear me in heaven? Can you see
that I've kept all the letters you wrote me? Can you hear Lucian
reading right now? I don't know if I'm on my way to see Jesus
and you right now. I'm scared. I don't want to leave Momma,
Rowan, and Eliza. I know it must have been very hard when you
were sick to know that it was almost time for you to go home even*

though you loved Jesus so much. You really inspired me. Both you and Momma are my best gifts. I'm so scared and I miss you and Momma. I'm trying to hold on to Jesus's hand. If you can hear me, Daddy, please pray for me. I love you. Isabella kept listening with all her heart as Lucian read.

"Our gathering here for your sixteenth birthday reflects our recognition of the fact that you are getting still closer to the time when you will be leaving your nest, your home. No matter where you go or what you do—the good and the bad, the successes and the failures—you will never drift so far away that you are not welcome to return. No matter what! Your nest, Isabella, is this home, and this family. Your nest is real love. Real love can withstand anything in life. Real love is never going to turn its back on you. Real love will follow you wherever you go. Just five weeks ago I was reading about Moses. That is an amazing story.

"Oh—has it been a while since you read about him? Well, let's go ahead and take a glimpse at his story right now. I pray your heart is encouraged. When Moses was talking with God at the burning bush, something amazing happened. Yes, it is quite amazing to know that God chose to talk with him that way. But something else amazing happened. It was a breakthrough."

Isabella vividly pictured herself reading those very words at the birthday party. She remembered that later that night after all the guests had left, she and her parents had sat down in the den and had a long conversation about the wonders of Moses's story. That was one of the most incredible memories Isabella had to date: listening to both her parents sharing their walk of faith with her. It was a memory forever imprinted on her heart. Thinking perhaps there was a reason she was hearing those words right then, Isabella tried her best to listen, and hoped she wouldn't miss a word.

"Exodus 4:8 reads, 'Then the Lord said, "If they do not believe you or pay attention to the first miraculous sign, they may believe the second. But if they do not believe these two signs or listen to you, take some water from the Nile and pour it on the dry ground. The water you take from the river will become blood on the ground." Moses said to the Lord, "O Lord, I have never been eloquent, neither in the past nor since you have spoken to your servant. I am slow of speech and tongue." The Lord said to him, "Who gave man his mouth? Who makes him deaf or mute? Who gives him sight or makes him blind? Is it not I, the Lord? Now go; I will help you speak and will teach you what to say." But Moses said, "O Lord, please send someone else to do it."'

"Isabella, just as God chose Moses for a task, He has great plans for you too. On days when you feel the mountain in front of you or the fear plaguing you is too much, remember, God is with you. I know you've been carrying a heavy load for years. Sweetheart, you're not

meant to carry that weight alone. I know you're trying to do your best to have fun and enjoy life. I know. It hurts our hearts to know your heart's been hurting over losing Grandpa and your friends. It's normal to hurt. It's the process of grief. We're here with you, and we're cheering for you. Never apologize for feeling grief. Feeling is how you get through the pain."

A flashback of standing in the kitchen hugging both her parents when she heard the news of her grandfather dying filled her thoughts. Isabella knew she could not have gotten through that pain without God and her parents. Even with the love, she felt alone and had to trust that love would bring her through. She was feeling the same way now and believed deep inside it was no coincidence that those words were being spoken into her life again.

"Rest assured, sweet daughter, God has all your tears in a bottle. He knows every time you cry. He was with you then and He is with you now. Princess, He has great plans for you. Jeremiah 29:11–13 tells us, "For I know the plans I have for you," declares the Lord, "plans to prosper you and not to harm you, plans to give you hope and a future. Then you will call upon me and come and pray to me, and I will listen to you. You will seek me and find me when you seek me with all your heart." Never stop seeking Him. Ask Him to help restore your heart with joy. He will. If it hurts to ask, know that we're asking Him for you. We love you, sweetheart.

"Sweet sixteen. It's hard to believe my little girl is growing up so fast. Always remember that you, Isabella, are a masterpiece. It's true! You're a masterpiece created in love. Did you know that there are sixteen characteristics of love that the apostle Paul wrote about in First Corinthians 13:4–8? Yes, sixteen descriptions. I thought it would be fitting to include them in your birthday letter. I pray that not only on this day but on every day from here on, you will carry with you what love truly is. For it is this understanding that will enhance how you love and receive love. So, are you ready to be reminded of these truths? These are the descriptions of love Apostle Paul speaks of … powerful truths. 'Love is patient, love is kind. It does not envy, it does not boast, it is not proud. It is not rude, it is not self-seeking, it is not easily angered, it keeps no record of wrongs. Love does not delight in evil but rejoices with the truth. It always protects, always trusts, always hopes, always perseveres. Love never fails.'

"Isabella, always remember that you are greatly loved by the creator of the universe and by your family. You are remarkable in His sight! All He sees when He looks at you is love. Years from now when you're reading through your letters again—and I hope you read through them often—I pray you will be reminded of Ephesians 2:10, which reads, 'For we are God's workmanship, created in Christ Jesus to do good works which God prepared in advance for us to do.' He has

created us anew in Christ Jesus, so we can do the good
things He planned for us long ago.

"Hide these truths in your heart. Enjoy the journey,
Isabella! Remember to make a wish today—a wish
from your heart to God. May all your dreams and
hopes come true, Princess. Happy birthday! Love, Dad."

Wide awake on the inside, Isabella heard footsteps shuffling as if someone else was entering the room.

"Ciao, Lucian. How's our girl today?"

"Ciao, Dr. Impastato. Isabella's mom asked me to read these letters to Isabella. Maybe she can hear me."

"Maybe she can. I believe in miracles, you know. I'll come check on her later. Keep reading. Keep believing. Keep praying."

"Isabella, can you hear me? Can you hear me reading? I don't know how God does it. But this letter is ministering to me. Do you think that's sort of a miracle? I've been praying about a lot of things and reading your dad's words to you. The way he talks about trusting God, it's all—well, it's all incredible."

I can hear you. Lucian, I can hear you. Please don't stop reading. Please.

"God, it's me. Lucian."

Isabella wasn't sure if she was dreaming or if her ears were hearing Lucian praying. Soon she realized he was having a conversation with God all on his own, by her bedside. She pictured him with arms open wide and lifted up to the heavens.

"Here I am, Lord. It's been a while, I know. It's been five years since my Sophia went home to you. I still don't understand why you had to take her and our baby I never saw born. I don't want to resent you anymore. Will you please forgive me? Is it okay for me to start having feelings for someone again? Am I disrespecting you and Sophia? I like Isabella, and I'm really worried about her. You're a good Father. Help her, Lord. Increase my faith like you increased the Apostle Paul's faith, and please help me to do right by Isabella. In your name I pray. Amen."

Weeping from deep inside at the sincerity of Lucian's prayer, Isabella's heart was melting. She didn't hear anything else for the rest of the night.

"Ciao, Isabella. It's Lucian." Hearing Lucian whisper woke Isabella. Although she didn't react physically, on the inside she became instantly alert.

Lucian. You came back! You really came back! I'm awake. I really am. Can you see my fingers moving yet?

"I have another birthday letter to read to you. I don't have to clock in for another few hours, so I definitely have time to spare. So, what do you say? How about another birthday letter reading?"

Yes, please!

"*Happy twentieth birthday! Can you remember the letter you got on your thirteenth birthday? Your thoughts were I'm a big kid now. I can babysit my three-year-old sister and brother. Boys? Yuck! Who needs them! Yeah, I think that's called growing up. So, where are we now in your book of life? Many interesting journeys have taken place through the storybook of Isabella, wouldn't you say? You made it through your freshman year in college! Much joy as well as much heartache has brought you to where you are now. It's all been part of the unique tapestry unfolding that God Himself has designed.*

"Your mother and I know that this past year
has brought about new challenges—gut-wrenching
challenges. Sweetheart, that's part of life. Life can get
messy at times. Be encouraged that God, the One who
loves you more than you can fathom, is majestic, and
He delights in restoring joy. He brings unspeakable
joy. His character and faithfulness is not based on our
ever-changing circumstances. He can be trusted. From
where I'm standing, you look like you're doing just fine.

"Many times over this past year we have wished
that certain events hadn't taken place. But you know
what? You came through. Many times we wanted
to spare you from disappointment. But you know
what? You came through. Many times your heart got
disappointed when things didn't turn out the way you
hoped. But you know what? You came through. Yes
indeed, Princess, God's hand is upon you.

"I was going to write this letter Saturday so I would
be sure to have it done, but I wasn't in the mood to
write. My spirits were down, and I just wasn't quite
with it. But that's okay. We all have those days. Days
when nothing seems to go right. Days when we don't
want to talk to anybody, when our plans go wrong and
we're disappointed. Life does that to us a lot, doesn't
it? I know, Isabella, that you have had plans that
have gone wrong. You've hoped for things that never
happened. You've set your heart on something, only

to be disappointed. I might be wrong, daughter, but I think that is what's known as growing up."

I do have days like that, Dad. I have a lot of them. I just really miss having you here with us. We miss you so much. Makes my heart hurt for Momma, and sometimes I'm afraid of growing up. I don't want Mom to ever think I don't need her. Can you see me from heaven? Am I doing a good job growing up? God, can you let Dad know I'm listening to the letters?

"Writing this letter, I'm reminded about the story of Jabez in the Bible. Remember him? He prayed one of the most magnificent prayers recorded in scripture. Let's take a look at the prayer again. First Chronicles 4:9 reads, 'Jabez was more honorable than his brothers. His mother had named him Jabez, saying, "I gave birth to him in pain."

"'Jabez cried out to the God of Israel, "Oh, that you would bless me and enlarge my territory! Let your hand be with me, and keep me from harm so that I will be free from pain. And God granted his request.' My daughter, Jabez reached out to God. He chose to believe God would pay attention to him. He chose to believe he mattered. He chose to believe he was more than just a reminder of pain. Not only that, but he asked to be someone of influence for God. He dared to believe he was chosen to do so.

"Isabella, dare to ask God for blessings of favor as you shine for Him. Dare to ask Him for boldness as you

*speak of His goodness. Remember, we are not called
to persuade others to accept the Lord into their lives.
No, Princess, it's never been about convincing. We are
called to share the gospel … and by doing so, hearts will
be directed toward Him. The past 365 days have been
filled with many ups and downs. I know that you are
doing your best to stay positive. It's just in you to share
joy. My daughter, I want to remind you of the freedom
you have to let go. It's okay to cry. Crying brings
healing. I know that the other day you heard someone
say that you shouldn't cry."*

The words Lucian read aloud were once again speaking directly to her soul. Isabella had had to face times when people had told her she should be healthier. Those assumptions had served as triggers that sent her spiraling into anxious episodes. The two people Isabella confided in the most were her parents, and right now she wished she were back in the comforts of home. But somehow deep inside she knew God had her exactly where He wanted her. So she kept listening as Lucian read.

*"You were even told that you should be over the
losses that you've had by now. Your mom and I know it
hurt to hear someone you considered a friend tell you
that. I want you to know that God holds all our tears.
One may question why I would bring up something
so serious in a birthday letter. Well, it's real life, and
together, with God in the center, we can face any
obstacle and climb any mountain. Even in the most
difficult circumstances you've already faced, God was*

there. In the fun times, God was there. You know what? He's not leaving! Isn't that good news?

"I have found tremendous encouragement in Isaiah 41:10, which reads, 'So do not fear, for I am with you; do not be dismayed, for I am your God. I will strengthen you and help you; I will uphold you with my righteous right hand.' May the words encourage you, Princess. Yes, He wants us to live an abundant life! Yes, He wants us to have joy! Yes, He wants us to celebrate our birthday … and yes, He wants us to cling to Him.

"Today, my wish is that you will forgive yourself. Sweet daughter, you have not caused any circumstances that have taken loved ones from your life. Sweet daughter, it's okay to cry. Sweet daughter, there is hope. Hold tightly to God's hand. He will lead you on mighty adventures! Walk closely with Him. Remember, He is the One who tells the moon when to rise. Remember when you used to talk about moon strings? Remember what it was like to believe anything is possible? He holds the strings to your very life and He will never let go. Oh, the wonders and joys He has planned for you. The sun will rise again, daughter and it will shine like you. Make a wish, Isabella. Look at the candles on your cake and make a wish. There are still great, tremendous, fantastic, amazing days ahead of you!

"Daughter, do me a favor. All these years I've kept a journal of how you, Rowan, and Eliza have grown. You are all growing up so fast! You all have given me

incredible stories to share just by how you are living life. I'm going to need something really good to write about in your last letter next year, something to make it really special. It will be your final one, so I'll need to write about something really outstanding. I know that for this coming year, I would like you to just be yourself. Happy birthday! Love, Dad.

"Beautiful message, Isabella. I hope your heart heard every word. I have to go now but will come by later. God be with you, friend."

Thank you so much, Lucian. I heard every word. Please keep praying for me. Isabella then drifted off to sleep once more.

Chapter 9

"Isabella, can you hear me? Some people are here to see you. Little Giselle wants you to know she has a panettone for you and everyone in your office. She's on her way to bring it to the clinic."

Isabella heard loud, deep coughing and then Giselle's voice. "Can I have a few minutes alone with her, Dad? Please?"

"Sure, sweetheart. We'll be right by the door."

Isabella envisioned Giselle standing by her bed and thought it one of the sweetest and tender moments ever.

"Dear God, please heal my new friend, Ms. Isabella. She was in a big car accident. She needs you right now. I know that you can do anything. You created the sun, the moon, and the stars. Are you holding up the moon by strings? I bet you are. Anyway, I know in my heart that nothing is too hard for you. Not even healing somebody. Can you please make Ms. Isabella feel better? She's been sleeping for a while now, and Mr. Lucian misses her. Her family back home is praying for her too. They're sad. Can you please hug them right now? Can you please tell them everything will be okay?"

Hearing Giselle pray, Isabella began to weep. *Can they see me crying, God? Can they hear me weeping? Please wake me up. Am I ever going to wake up? Please God, help me.* Isabella continued listening to Giselle's voice.

"Jesus, I know that you can heal anybody. I already know why you're not going to heal me. I know that you're ready to take me back home. I'm ready to see you too. Please help Papa and Mama not be sad for too long when you take me. I want them to keep dancing. But for Ms. Isabella, I bet there's more that you want her to do here, so can you please heal her? Please wake her up and make her happy. Thank you, Jesus. I love you."

"Thank you so much for the prayers, Giselle. You are an angel. I'm sure she knows you and your family were here."

"Thank you, Mr. Lucian, for letting me pray. I have to go now. But I'll keep Isabella in my prayers."

"Isabella, can you hear me? Did you hear Giselle's prayer? We're all praying for you."

Isabella had definitely heard every word. She tried to move her left finger, hoping Lucian would see.

"Isabella, did you just move your finger? Can you hear me? You know, we've got a lunch date you have to take me on. I'm holding you to that. God loves you, Isabella. Find peace in Him through all this. You're not alone. I have another letter from your dad here. How about I read it now?"

Yes, please! I'm ready.

"Happy twenty-first birthday, Isabella! When I think back over your childhood, I guess the one picture that stands out in my mind is the time that your mother and I took you on your first beach vacation. You had the prettiest and biggest smile, along with the sweetest laugh. Pure joy. After watching you grow and develop over the past twenty-one years that same picture stands out as the true Isabella, the mark that shows your attitude toward life and has carried you

through a lot of rough times. You've had to change schools a number of times. Each time, you had to pick up your roots, leave your friends behind, start all over, and adjust to new surroundings, new friends, and new situations. You pressed on through these changes with your positive attitude even though many times life felt like a roller coaster."

Isabella remembered writing her feelings about a roller coaster in the prayer book in the chapel a few days earlier. Instantly she began weeping at the timing of writing the prayer and hearing the letter. Both her parents had known how hard it was for her back then as she tried to process grief. Isabella felt the same way now. All she could think was that God might be winking at her in this moment. Oh yes, she sensed God in her midst.

"Your mother and I can still see that same attitude, Isabella. Attitude, faith, and courage! That's you! Well, I guess this is it, Isabella—your last letter. You are all grown up now. Where has the time gone, Princess? I know you've saved these letters over the years, and I hope you take them with you wherever you go in the future. I've never been one for saying how I feel out loud. But I've tried to tell you, Rowan, and Eliza how I feel by way of writing.

"I remember a few letters back, telling you to never stop fighting. Never stop fighting the good fight of faith. Never. Take these letters, Isabella, and put them in your heart. They are the ones that tell you how much

you're loved. When your mom and I have passed on to glory, you will always be able to glance back in time by reading these pages. When you look back, and I hope you will look back often, remember how much we loved you."

Memories rushed in of family Christmases spent celebrating the miracle of Jesus and the love of family. Christmas music would echo through the house as presents were opened. Isabella's mom always served bacon, scrambled eggs, and biscuits seasoned with white gravy for breakfast. Relatives would come over in the afternoon, eat ham with all the fixings, and dine on other deliciously prepared food. Biscuits with white gravy, baked macaroni and banana pudding. Isabella would give anything to be able to eat right now. And she would give anything to be able to do that again with her entire family. *Yes, Daddy,* her heart cried. *I'll remember to look back often.*

"My daughter, be vigilant about reading scripture. It's the best love letter you will ever read. God wrote it for you—for all of us. What a book! Stories of kings and queens, triumphs, tragedies, wars, and victories. Stories of surrender, redemption, restoration, and salvation. A love letter like none other. On this, your twenty-first birthday, my prayer is that you will hold on to fierce faith as you step into the next chapter of your life—a faith like that of King Jehoshaphat. Remember his story? Let's go back and read about him together, right now.

"Scripture tells us in Second Chronicles 20:1–9 that King Jehoshaphat had a vast army coming against him. The Moabites and Ammonites wanted to destroy him. The king did not turn away from God. He sought His protection with fierce faith. My prayer is that you will forever have fierce faith, Isabella. It is quite amazing to read about what King Jehoshaphat said as he stood up in the assembly of Judah and Jerusalem at the temple of the Lord. He prayed, 'O Lord, God of our fathers, are you not the God who is in heaven? You rule over all the kingdoms of the nations. Power and might are in your hand, and no one can withstand you. O our God, did you not drive out the inhabitants of this land before your people Israel and give it forever to the descendants of Abraham your friend? They have lived in it and have built in it a sanctuary for your Name, saying, "If calamity comes upon us, whether the sword of judgment, or plague or famine, we will stand in your presence before this temple that bears your Name and will cry out to you in our distress, and you will hear us and save us."'

"Isabella, the Lord will never leave you. He has already set wonders in motion to bring unspeakable joy your way! His plans are good. An amazing adventure awaits you! Fill yourself with the promises God Himself has written to you. They will sustain you. When life gets tough, reach for the Bible again. Hold it close to your heart. King Jehoshaphat prayed in Second

Chronicles 20:12, 'O our God, will you not judge them? For we have no power to face this vast army that is attacking us. We do not know what to do, but our eyes are upon you.'

"Isabella, always keep your eyes on God, especially when you feel a battle is right in front of you. Whatever that battle may be, keep your eyes on God. Now, let's read what the Holy Spirit said to Jahaziel, who was standing with King Jehoshaphat and many others in the assembly. Second Chronicles 20:15 refers to the Holy Spirit saying, "'Listen, King Jehoshaphat and all who live in Judah and Jerusalem! This is what the Lord says to you: 'Do not be afraid or discouraged because of this vast army. For the battle is not yours, but God's. Tomorrow march down against them. They will be climbing up by the Pass of Ziz, and you will find them at the end of the gorge in the Desert of Jeruel. You will not have to fight this battle. Take up your positions; stand firm and see the deliverance the Lord will give you, O Judah and Jerusalem. Do not be afraid; do not be discouraged. Go out to face them tomorrow, and the Lord will be with you.'" Isn't it amazing to know this is a true story? It's an incredible story!"

Isabella's heart reached out to God. *Why do I worry so much, God? Why do I let anxiety get the best of me? I don't want to disappoint you. I remember Mom and Dad always telling me that it's okay to cry. They always told me you would help me feel better. I need you now, God, because I'm scared like I've never been before. Please speak to me through Dad's letters. I know you're having me hear them again for a reason.*

"Here's my favorite part! Second Chronicles 20:21 reads, 'After consulting the people, Jehoshaphat appointed men to sing to the Lord and to praise him for the splendor of his holiness as they went out at the head of the army, saying: "Give thanks to the Lord, for his love endures forever."' My precious daughter, King Jehoshaphat marched into battle with his army singing praises to the Lord. When they reached the enemy, the battle was already over, for they had turned on one another. The Lord moved mightily that day and honored the praises of His children.

"That same God loves you and will always go before you. Press on with joy, hope, fierce faith, and courage, Isabella! You are a mighty warrior! One more thing: remember to look up often, with childlike faith, at the moon and stars. Yes, the creator of the universe spoke those into existence. Every time you look up at the moon in wonder, be reminded of those three verses that speak of His creation. I listed them here for you. Oh, how great is our God! Psalm 19:1: 'The heavens declare the glory of God, and the sky above proclaims his handiwork.' Psalm 148:3: 'Praise Him, sun and moon, praise Him, all you shining stars!' Psalm 89:37: 'Like the moon it shall be established forever, a faithful witness *in the skies.' May God's richest blessings chase you, my daughter! Happy birthday, Princess! Love, Dad."*

At the moment he spoke of the king standing firm in battle, Isabella, who could hear every word, remembered her dream. *That's in my dream! That's in my dream, God!*

Chapter 10

"Can you hear me, Isabella? It's Lucian. What a beautiful gift you've been given with these letters. I can't stop thinking about them. This week is surprising me in many ways. I never expected events to turn out the way they have with us. I certainly never expected the honor of reading your dad's letters to you. I so deeply hope you can hear me. Your mom wants you to know she'll be here soon. I've been keeping her updated every day."

I can hear you. I love hearing you read the letters. Please read more. Please tell Mom I love her. Oh how Isabella wished she could hear her mom right now. She believed Lucian's heart was being moved by the letters' messages. In that moment, Isabella realized that by allowing the accident to occur, God had presented this situation for a reason and Lucian would receive encouragement as well. Maybe, she figured, her dream about standing still as she decided whether to take a step was about not being afraid to share her story with others. Maybe it meant that even if others couldn't relate to specific events in her life, Isabella could relate to stories of others facing pain. Maybe that's what she was supposed to do: rise up with an army of believers and encourage others to focus on the light of God's grace that causes the dark forces to flee.

"How about another letter, Isabella? I left the other page of this letter back at your house. I'm so sorry. But I can read the second half to you. I hope you enjoy it.

"This year you have asked us many questions about your faith. Never stop asking for and seeking the Father's wisdom. God knows all, and He is the One from whom all wisdom comes. We will continue to try to guide you, Rowan, and Eliza in truth. You are quickly approaching the time when you will go to college. We hope we've prepared you well for the journey ahead.

"Isabella, if there's one thing we can say as you prepare for this next chapter of your life, it is this: you must use your Christianity as a foundation upon which to base all your decisions. Some of these decisions, I assure you, will be very difficult. In all too short a time you will be going out into the world by yourself. My one prayer is that your mother and I have given you the training, guidance, and love you need. I think you have been an excellent student of life for the past eighteen years, and I think you will do just fine. In case I forgot to tell you, we're very proud of you. Do me a favor, daughter. As you travel through your future, keep your eyes open wide enough to see all the beauty there is and your heart open wide enough to feel all the love there is too. Every once in a while, glance over your shoulder at your eighteenth birthday and hear us saying, 'Happy eighteenth birthday!" Wow, Isabella, eighteen years.

This is just the beginning of your great adventure! We love you, lady!"

Soon Isabella heard other voices in the room.

"How's our Isabella, Lucian?"

"Thanks for checking on her, Hattie. I'm reading her birthday letters that her dad wrote."

"I know about those letters. I was standing by her in the airport when she thought they were lost. I'm so glad you can read them to her. God is good."

"May I read the letter?" Isabella recognized Francesca's voice.

God, please speak to Francesca somehow through Dad's letter.

"Sure. This is only part of a letter. There are many more. She's really been blessed to have such a gift like this. I wish I had something like this from my dad."

Isabella wasn't afraid of dying. She had accepted Jesus as her Lord and Savior and knew heaven's door awaited her. But God wasn't ready to take her home yet. There was more work for her to do on earth and more work to be done inside her. Although she was afraid the process of weeding out fear, pride, and guilt would hurt, she wanted to heal. Way down deep inside, Isabella wanted to find peace.

"Let's pray for our friend," Isabella heard Hattie suggest. Then there was some shuffling in the room, and Isabella imagined they were forming a circle.

Hattie began to pray. "Dear Lord Jesus, we lift up our dear sister in Christ, Isabella. We know You have her and are in control. We know these circumstances are not a surprise to You. We also know that it is not by chance that we are all standing here right now, united as one. We're asking for a miracle. We're asking for Your healing hand to touch Isabella. Wake her, Lord, from this coma. We ask for divine healing. We ask for her eyesight to not be affected. We ask for all brain function to be restored.

"We know You created the heavens and the earth. The stars are too numerous to count. The sun and moon You can still with one breath. You are mighty. You hold us in Your hands just as You are holding the heavens. Nothing is out of step, and what You have set in motion will not be thrown off course.

"With that declaration of belief, hear our hearts' plea, Lord. You said in Jeremiah for us to call out to You. We're calling out to You now. We pray for comfort for all her family and friends back home who are worried and in great distress. They are still trying to accept the shock of losing their friend Brendan. Comfort them, Lord. Hold them close. We pray for them to feel a calmness right now. Lord, surround them with Your grace. Envelop them with the love, comfort, and peace only You can provide. It is in Your mighty name, Jesus, that we pray. Amen."

A calmness came over Isabella. In her mind she envisioned herself walking hand in hand with Jesus. As they were walking, a mountainous range appeared before them. Isabella wasn't sure if she was dreaming or passing on into glory. She looked at Jesus and knew it was time to let go. Time to let go of fear. Time to truly grasp the beauty of God's promises and the birthday letters that chronicled how her mighty savior had always been moving in her life for good. Isabella envisioned Jesus weeping with her and was reminded that heaven had never overlooked her pain.

As Jesus and Isabella stood before the mountain, Jesus pointed to the valley. Isabella saw a vast crowd of people praying on their knees. As she looked to Jesus for revelation, she heard Him tell her to go and inspire. Isabella prayed again for God to wake her up. Then she heard an unfamiliar voice coming from the hall.

"Excuse me, sir. My name is Guiseppe. I don't mean to invade your privacy. This is my second day on the job. I'm caring for the patient in the next room. As I was walking down the hall yesterday, I heard you reading to Isabella. I asked God to give me a sign if He was real and still loved me. Then I saw you again and knew I had to mention the letters."

"Ciao, Guiseppe. My name is Lucian. Congratulations on your new job. Yes, I was just about to visit with Isabella. Please pray for her. God's always listening to us, and it's powerful when two or more agree in prayer."

Her heart moved with compassion, Isabella listened as Lucian encouraged Guiseppe. She believed this moment was not coincidental either.

"I've been a mess for a long time," Guiseppe said. "I haven't been a good dad. I moved away and have not spoken to my son and daughter in three years. I moved to Rome to be close to them. Maybe to start over. But I don't know if they will welcome me back."

"Guiseppe, the Lord ordains our steps. He rejoices in restoration. I will pray for you and your family. I'm here to tell you that Jesus delights when hearts come to Him. We do not have to be cleaned up to seek His salvation. We are called to come as we are."

Isabella heard Guiseppe weeping. "Lucian, how do I get right with God?"

"Listen to what the Apostle Paul wrote in Romans 6:1–14." Isabella heard shuffling and assumed it was Lucian opening Bible pages.

"'What shall we say, then? Shall we go on sinning so that grace may increase? By no means! We died to sin; how can we live it any longer? Or don't you know that all of us who were baptized into Christ Jesus were baptized into his death? We were therefore buried with him through baptism into death in order that, just as Christ was raised from the dead through the glory of the Father, we too may live a new life. If we have been united with him like this in his death, we will certainly also be united with him in his resurrection. For we know that our old self was crucified with him so that the body of sin might be done away with, that we should no longer be slaves to sin—because anyone who has died has been freed from sin. Now if we died with Christ, we believe that we will also live with him. For we know that since Christ was raised from the dead, he cannot die again; death no longer has mastery over him. The death he died, he died to sin once for all; but the life he lives, he lives to God. In the same way, count yourselves dead to sin but alive to God in Christ Jesus. Therefore do not let sin reign in your mortal body so that you obey its evil desires. Do not offer the parts of your body to sin, as instruments of wickedness, but rather offer yourselves to God, as those who have been brought from death to life; and offer the parts of your body to him as instruments of righteousness. For sin shall not be your master, because you are not under law, but under grace.'"

"How should I pray, Lucian? I want Jesus in my life."

"Amen, my brother. Amen."

As Guiseppe wept tenderly, Isabella sensed any shackles that had a grip on him being loosed. Seeing with her mind's eye what was happening—a soul about to pray for forgiveness—Isabella was astonished. Never had she expected that out of a circumstance such as this, God would arrange for a soul to be set free. She was in complete awe and wonder of the miraculous working power of Jesus.

"Guiseppe, repeat after me: Dear Lord Jesus."

Believing it was an invitation for her as well, Isabella rededicated herself to the Lord, repeating the words of the prayer in her head right along with Lucian.

Dear Lord Jesus.

"I'm a sinner."

I'm a sinner.

"Today I'm asking for Your forgiveness."

Today I'm asking for Your forgiveness.

"I believe You died on the cross for my sins and that You rose again."

I believe You died on the cross for my sins and that You rose again.

"I'm asking for You to help me turn away from my sins. I invite You into my heart and life. Wash me clean. Create a new heart in me."

I'm asking for You to help me turn away from my sins. I invite You into my heart and life. Wash me clean. Create a new heart in me.

Isabella sensed her own soul being stirred. With all that was within her, she believed the Holy Spirit was in the room and in all the hearts present.

"I accept You today as my Lord and Savior. In Your name I pray. Amen."

I accept You today as my Lord and Savior. In Your name I pray. Amen.

After the prayer, Isabella's ears went silent to the sounds in the room. Her heart began to receive what she believed was revelation about her dream. Maybe the swords symbolized the mighty word of God piercing hearts with truth and triumphing over death? Maybe the concrete turning to grass in her dream was a reminder of Psalm 92, which spoke of singing praises to the Lord and having roots of faith stand firm like the tree in Lebanon? With that wonder, Isabella fell asleep with a renewed soul.

Chapter 11

"I'm here, Isabella. It's Momma. Everything's going to be all right. We love you." Isabella could hear her mom weeping. Tears fell directly on Isabella's hands.

Momma! You're here! I can hear you! I love you, Momma! God, please let Momma hear me. Please.

"Can you hear me, Bella? It's Eliza. I love you so much! Rowan is on his way and will be here tonight. We love you so much!"

Eliza! You're here too! I really can hear you! I love you! Just then Isabella's right hand began to twitch.

"Did she just move her hand? Momma, did Isabella just move her hand?"

Yes, I moved my hand! I love y'all so much, and I'm so scared. Please pray for me. I'm holding on to God's hand as best I can. Please pray for me. Isabella wept on the inside, wondering if she would ever be able to see her family again with her own eyes or would only be able to hear their voices, and if so, for how long. Then it hit her. She was reminded again of the power of God's grace that allowed her to survive the crash. Even more, she remembered the beauty of how her father's letters had ministered to her again and ministered to new hearts clear across the ocean. All her dreams began to make sense: she had taken the step of faith to move to Italy, and hearts had been touched by her life in ways she could never have imagined. Now Isabella wanted to wake up not just for the sake of waking up but with a renewed purpose—a purpose that needed to shine like a city on a hill for the Savior she adored.

Chapter 12

One year. It had been exactly one year since Isabella had been in the hospital. In fact, on the first anniversary of her waking up, she was sharing her testimony at church. Everything had come full circle, and Isabella would not have had it any other way. Not one step. That was the secret: knowing that our steps are ordained by the Lord and that absolutely nothing happens without His approval.

Isabella's dream was real and had purpose. She had a vision of raising an army for the Lord to fight the good fight of faith. She had a story to tell and a testimony to share. Isabella had a victory to shout, birthing purpose from pain. Isabella was marked. Isabella was blessed. Isabella was real. For the first time in her life, Isabella was becoming transparent. She was healing, and today she would share her testimony. Standing in the back of the church, she read the letter she'd started reading the year before, on the night of her birthday.

> *Princess,*
> *The clock of life is ticking much faster than your mother and I would like. The lullaby "Turn Around" sung by Malvina Reynolds has the words, "Where are you going, my little one?" This song, which I'm sure*

you have heard, talks about a parent's surprise at how quickly the daughter has grown. That song says what we feel. It felt strange, watching you leave for school this morning, knowing that we were watching our thirteen-year-old daughter going out the door. We have watched you go out the door to school for eight years, so we should be used to it by now. Where have all the years gone? The song goes on to say, "Turn around and you're a young girl," and today we turn. Your birthday is a signal for us to turn around and see how much you've grown. You've grown a lot. You've grown into a beautiful, bright, independent young lady, of whom we are quite proud.

Your mother and I are in a race with time. In the precious years between now and when you have babes of your own, we want to give you all the love, support, guidance, advice, and respect that we possibly can. One day you will be going out on your own, and we will quietly back into the shadows of your life, confidently watching you trying your own wings. But before we back away, we're going to do our best to let you know that we are here.

"Where are you going, my little one?" This is a question that no one can answer right now. None of us can predict what your future holds. But your mother and I both feel that you have the faith, perseverance, courage, and determination to make the best of

whatever life hands you. "Turn around and you're a young girl." We're turning around and looking, Isabella. We like what we see.

We wish, Princess that we could go with you every time you walk out the door. We wish we could always be there to protect and lead you. Obviously, we cannot do that. Life is a process of growing up, of walking out the door on your own. You have shown us, Isabella that you know how to handle yourself as you hold tightly to God's hand. "Where are you going, my little one?" You are walking through the door of adolescence and one day through the door of young adulthood.

Princess, hold on to your faith tightly. Be encouraged by what God's Word tells us. His book, the love letter He wrote to us, is marvelous. When life gets tough, remember standing on the deck with your mom and me, talking about moon strings. In fact, hide the psalms in your heart and let them speak peace. Let them remind you that God created all and nothing happens that is out of His control.

Oh yes, sweet daughter, He created the heavens and the earth. He has a wonderful plan. His love for you is everlasting. He rejoices over you. He fills us with joy. If that joy is ever quenched by heartache and you feel ill equipped for the battle, remember the armor that He provides for you in His Word. What a mighty armor it is. Ephesians 6:10–17 tells us, "Finally, be strong in the

Lord and in his mighty power. Put on the full armor of
God so that you can take your stand against the devil's
schemes. For our struggle is not against flesh and blood,
but against the rulers, against the authorities, against
the spiritual forces of evil in the heavenly realms.
Therefore put on the full armor of God, so that when
the day of evil comes, you may be able to stand your
ground, and after you have done everything, to stand.
Stand firm then, with the belt of truth buckled around
your waist, with the breastplate of righteousness in
place, and with your feet fitted with the readiness
that comes from the gospel of peace. In addition to all
this, take up the shield of faith, with which you can
extinguish all the flaming arrows of the evil one. Take
the helmet of salvation and the sword of the Spirit,
which is the word of God." Your strength comes from
Him. Be encouraged that He will be with you always,
Isabella. Always!

"Turn around." Don't forget, Isabella, to turn
around often. Every time you turn, you will see us. We
may not be there physically, but I assure you that we
will always be standing with you in spirit. As my pen
glides along this page, my heart is reminded that this is
the beginning of a new chapter. I pray that in years to
come, these words will comfort, encourage, and inspire
you. You are dearly loved, Isabella, by your heavenly
Father and by your family. We are so proud of you! Step
into your next chapter with great anticipation, wonder,

and above all, childlike faith. Your mom and I love you
to the moon and back! Happy birthday, Princess!
   Love, Dad

Isabella's tears fell upon the pages. That was the first time in seven years she had finished reading her first birthday letter—a symbol of a new chapter. "I miss you, Daddy. Love you," she said softly. A few minutes later Isabella was reminded about her dream. Clarity came rushing in. The Holy Spirit was quickening her about God's word, about His promises, about His power, about His faithfulness to speak truth to her back then and the hope and promise that He was speaking to her now. Isabella clutched the letter tightly to her chest as healing tears of joy streamed down her cheeks.

Gloria, Eliza, Rowan, and Annalise walked up to the front so they would be sitting by Isabella. They saved seats for Lucian, Hattie, Francesca, Gianna and Guiseppe. Before walking toward the front of the church, Isabella noticed her reflection in the glass door of the main entrance. The sunlight was reflected on her left shoulder, and she took it as a sign that God's hand was upon her like it had always been. Taking a deep breath, she proceeded to walk into the sanctuary. Looking at the podium where she would soon be standing was surreal.

Isabella took a seat in the last row. With head bowed she closed her eyes. *Be with me here, Jesus. I can't do this without you. I don't know if I'm ready for this, God. What if I skip lines when I'm reading? What if my hands start to shake from being nervous? Give me courage, Lord. Give me strength. I love you.*

Over the next half hour, the church, which could seat two hundred comfortably, was filled to capacity. After greeting family and friends, Isabella was as ready as she would ever be.

"Hello, my name is Isabella Cole. I am a grateful believer in the Lord Jesus Christ, and my primary area of recovery is grief and loss. Thank you in advance for listening to my story. I was raised in a loving home in New Orleans as the oldest of three children. As a child I loved to be silly, tell funny jokes, and make people laugh."

Seeing her family seated in the front row was invaluable. Of all the people in the room, her mom, Rowan, and Eliza were the ones she most wanted there. Isabella noticed her mom pointing to a piece of white paper on the empty chair beside her. Isabella adjusted her reading glasses to focus on the words written on it: "Dad's chair." Isabella said the words softly and had to put down the microphone. The audience was silent.

"Excuse me. I just noticed the chair my family set aside in honor of my dad. I'm getting choked up already."

Shouts of "You're doing great!" and "God's with you!" from the audience echoed throughout the room. After a brief pause, Isabella courageously continued.

"At five years old I began attending children's church, where I met many wonderful friends. It was around that time that I became fascinated with the idea of God holding the moon by three strings. In fact, I used to tell my parents that God must have been holding the moon. I imagined the three strings symbolized the Father, Son, and Holy Spirit. My faith was real. Childlike. I believed anything was possible. I also kept praying for a baby brother or sister. Praying, praying, and more praying. I would constantly ask my parents to have another baby. I never stopped asking! One Valentine's Day, my mom and dad gave me a gift to open. I jumped for joy when I saw twin set baby booties inside! I was so excited! To my delight, Rowan and Eliza were born when I was ten years old. It was really cool to have twins in the house!"

Isabella looked at her mom and smiled. Although she tried

to hold back her tears, she wasn't able to do it. This time they were happy tears.

"Whenever someone walks into my mom's house, they say it feels peaceful. I feel the same way. God's there. Real love is there. Acceptance is there. Hope is there. But even with all the love around me, my soul was not immune to pain and heartache. My parents did the best they could to encourage me to grow in faith and trust God. To this day I remain immensely thankful for them. I had no idea that soon my life would be interrupted by great loss.

"Between the ages of eleven and nineteen, I had to say goodbye to seven people. It was way too soon to lose family and close friends. My life was falling apart. I was shattered on the inside and didn't realize that the glue I needed was there all along. Car accidents. Illnesses. Tragedies. I have continued to lose many more loved ones as an adult. Although I won't reveal every experience in detail here, I will share an overview of how these losses have affected my life and how I believe God's grace has always been with me."

Isabella looked down at the pages in her hand. She just had to take a minute. This was a big moment. She knew that healing was taking place. "Okay, I'm ready. I can do this," she said, looking at Lucian. "The year I turned thirteen brought grief mixed with tremendous guilt. I was devastated thinking I had something to do with it. On the bus ride home from middle school one day, I saw my friend walking home, carrying her school books. I quickly remembered that I was supposed to walk home with her so we could finish an art project." Isabella paused, holding back tears, and looked down at her hands on the podium, to refocus and regain control. Then she continued.

"My friend took her own life that night. I began struggling with the notion that if I had walked home with her, maybe she would still be here. That was a very difficult time. I clung tightly to God, my parents, and my friends. That was when a heavy weight of guilt came over me. It stuck with me even though I tried to get back to having a normal life—well, what I thought would be considered normal. I didn't want to think about what had happened, because if I did, the hurt would become real again. I would be reminded that the event really had taken place.

"Through those tough times, God was continuing to bring joyful moments into my life. Family vacations, playing outside with friends, summer youth camp, and after-school clubs were bringing much happiness my way. That's what I tried to focus on. I enjoyed being silly with family. Swimming at the YMCA was one of my favorite pastimes. I really enjoyed church a lot too."

Then the all-too-familiar feeling of dizziness came upon her. Trying to suppress the urge to dash off the stage and hide, Isabella desperately prayed silently that she would not faint. Feeling cold and hot at the same time, she grabbed her water bottle, hoping the audience would not catch on to what was happening.

"One of my favorite memories of growing up is when my dad began the tradition of writing birthday letters to me, my brother, and my sister. We received our first letter when we turned thirteen and our final letter at the age of twenty-one. I have vivid memories of standing in our living room and reading the letters to a room full of family and friends. I treasure those moments. Something in the way the letters were written— the way God guided my dad's pen to speak about faith, hope, dreams, and reassuring love—brought everyone to tears. My dad always kept a journal with him. He recorded our life events. That is simply amazing to me. What a blessing."

Right then Isabella's throat began to tighten. The fresh hurt of grief is real for her, and in that moment she felt it strongly. Although almost four years has gone by since her father's death, it is still hard. She's still processing Brendan's loss too. Grief, Isabella knows, does not have a time limit. She's learning the beauty of keeping memories alive and the joy that can be found in recalling good times. Most important, she knows she will see loved ones again in heaven. Seeing her mom wink at her, Isabella placed her hand over her heart and winked back. Boosted by the encouragement and the love in her mother's eyes, Isabella continued.

"I lost my friend just a couple of years after I lost my grandpa to Parkinson's disease. So painful. I remember clear as a bell what it was like when a hospital bed was placed in our home for my grandpa. I wanted him to joke with me like he used to. I wanted Grandpa to laugh and take out his teeth like he used to. By the way, that really used to embarrass me at first, but then he and my friends would just crack up laughing every time he did it. He was so funny!" Isabella started laughing and so did everyone in the room.

"It's good to laugh, isn't it? I knew God was with me through those experiences. I began asking God a lot of questions and wondering what really happens when someone passes away, because in the same year, I lost another loved one. It was a lot to go through. I remember riding home in the car from my grandpa's funeral and watching the rain fall. I told my family, 'Grandpa must be crying from heaven, seeing all the people who loved him.'

"Hearing my mom sing in the choir was always a highlight, and I have amazing memories of my family singing together in Tennessee. I thank God for giving me those memories. But happy times soon were met with grief. My world turned upside down again. My friends and I were in shock. So many friends. If losing them wasn't hard enough, it was the way these events happened. My heart was shredded. That's the best way I can describe my pain. I remember sitting out on our deck, the very same place where I would look up at the sky believing that anything is possible with God. After all, He is the One who tells the sun and moon when to rise and set. I remember crying out for Him to hold me. I was scared. That's when fear began to creep into my young heart. I started becoming anxious whenever I heard someone was sick. I feared they would end up passing away too. I became anxious about being anxious."

Through pursed lips and a desperate heart, Isabella mumbled, "Give me strength, Lord." Then she continued reading. "After high school, I was excited about going to college. This was going to be a great new adventure. My freshman year: a brand new world full of possibilities. I remember one particular day when I got dressed up for class. Not for any particular reason. I just wanted to look pretty. That night I ran into my friend Matthew at a college baseball game. After we enjoyed catching up during the game, he wanted me to stay longer. I didn't stay. I went home. He never made it home."

The back of Isabella's neck became hot. Wondering if the audience was paying attention or at least not falling asleep, she looked up. All eyes were on her. The room was silent. Isabella sensed God was moving in and through her. In her heart she prayed. *Please help me finish strong, God. Please open their hearts to receive your hope through my testimony.* She continued with hope that her words would bring glory to God.

"Numb. That's exactly how I felt when I found out he had been killed in a car accident. Numb—a feeling that was becoming familiar. I found myself asking a familiar question. Could the situation have turned out differently if I had done something different? To this day I sometimes wonder what might have been had I stayed. But by God's grace, after all these years, I'm beginning to accept the truth that I was not responsible for his death or others.

"Although I tried to keep pressing on and really cling to my faith, the pain of so many losses was beginning to affect my personal life in more ways than one. My grades began to suffer, anxiety was building, and my temper was short. Dating relationships were not working out well, either. Life was messy. Today, as I look back, I can see that God was with me all along, and He's with me now. Compassion and empathy for others was filling my heart on a whole new level. I know it was one of God's ways of comforting me, holding on to me in the midst of a tornado of emotions. Reaching out to others and listening somehow ushered healing into my own heart. God was giving me strength to speak hope into others' lives. But I wasn't letting people fully get in to my world. I shared only to a certain point. If I talked too much, it hurt too much. I remember going to church more and looking at the altar, praying for understanding. My desperate heart wanted understanding. Desperate, that's who I was. Desperate, that's who I am. Desperate for God."

Taking a deep breath, Isabella was thankful to God for allowing her to speak with conviction about her own life story. She was thankful she hadn't passed out, and amazed by the strength inside to stand before others and share her story. Isabella knew this would not be the last time she would be called to give reason for her faith. She was ready.

"At age twenty-one, I was invited to a new church, a nondenominational one. When I walked in, I sensed true acceptance. I sensed true hope. I sensed the Savior. Words cannot fully describe what my church back home means to me. I love my new church here too. It brings great joy to my heart to say that when I decided to rededicate my life to Christ and get baptized as a new believer in Christ, my family shared that moment with me. I felt tremendous peace. I knew the Holy Spirit was with me. I knew it. I felt it.

"But then anxiety rushed through my veins, stealing the lifeblood within. It wasn't going to let go. As I entered my junior year of college, my dad was given a diagnosis of chronic obstructive pulmonary disorder."

Isabella recalled a time of deep prayer. That moment wasn't to be shared; it was just between her and Jesus. She had fallen to her knees one evening before bedtime, begging the Lord not to take her father. Crying in desperation, she had lifted prayers to heaven. Her tears exhausted her. An inner voice whispered that even though her father might be taken home soon, she would remain under the wings and protection of her heavenly father. It was then that Isabella looked over at her Bible, which happened to be open to Psalm 91. She began reading about God's promise of forever covering her under His wings and sending angels to guard her always. The tug on her heart was strong as she remembered the story she was still keeping just between her and Jesus. After a deep breath and sip of water, Isabella picked up the microphone again.

"My anxiety was off the charts now. Immeasurable. I was still trying to live a normal life. Trying. Every day. Trying. You see, my parents had always been there for me, encouraging me, loving me, and listening to me. Now, my anchor was not feeling well. My mom, with all the love she had inside, tried her best to prepare me, to help me accept what was happening to my dad. I just wouldn't accept it. He couldn't leave us yet. I wasn't ready. Not at all. My dad had to wear a portable oxygen tank. That never stopped him. He continued speaking at colleges, inspiring many about the importance of good health and not wasting any day.

"In the midst of trying to accept this new reality, I lost three more people within a couple of years: two former classmates and a family friend. They were all separate events. It was then that overanalyzing became part of my world. I overanalyzed everything. It was unhealthy, but I didn't know that. I was still going to school, still enjoying church, and still battling a secret fear of anxiety. It would not be too long before we would find out that a family friend who also had a lung condition would undergo lung transplant surgery and pass away on the table. We were stunned. Deeply saddened.

"I became even more anxious about Dad and terrified at the thought of losing him. I was holding on to hope. I was scared. Looking back now, I can see that I really was in denial, which came out through anger and fear.

"Christmas of 2005 holds a unique memory. My entire family was in town, and Dad, who actually looked better than he had in a long time, gave a wonderful speech and blessing over our family. Now I know deep inside that we were given a gift by God—a divine chance, a true gift, to be able to spend my dad's last moments on this earthly plane with him. On the Sunday morning just four days after Christmas, my dad was headed to the hospital unexpectedly to have his lungs drained. I thought I would see him soon and watch the Saints game with him. Within minutes my mom called. Dad wasn't going to make it. We needed to get to the hospital quickly."

Isabella saw her mother lean over in a sob. Something was connecting with Gloria deeply. Memories could be so bittersweet. Pausing for a moment, Isabella stepped away from the podium and walked over to her mom.

"Love you, Momma. Love you so much."

"Love you too. God's with you, sweetheart."

Standing back at the podium Isabella bravely continued. "My mom, brother, sister, and I all rode together to the hospital. The drive was only five minutes, but in reality it felt like forever. I was numb. When we got to the ICU, I asked my brother to fix Daddy's blanket, which had started to fall off the bed toward the floor. I didn't want him to get cold. My mind wasn't computing that Dad was dying. My heart wasn't either. When the hospital chaplain came in, I almost fainted. The reality of what was happening was just too much. As more family and friends began to arrive, I became weaker, nauseated, terrified. Through God's favor, Dad's doctor allowed our family and friends, now totaling ten people, to stand near the bedside and in the walkway. The nurses also came by Dad's room and joined hands with us. The staff kept telling our family how much they loved Dad. I just couldn't take it. It didn't feel real. I was certain Dad was just sleeping and later that night we would talk about the day.

"But Dad wasn't going to be back at home that night. He wasn't going to sit in the leather recliner and talk with us. He wasn't going to have dinner with us. He wasn't going to tell me about how important it was to never waste a day. Mom encouraged us all to join hands as she began to sing a hymn. When she did, my dad's heart rate began to go up and down. I was weeping and smiling at the same time. My emotions were all over the place. My anchor was going home. Oh how my heart wept as I looked at Mom's face as she said goodbye to her beloved. I remember hearing us tell Daddy it was okay to go home as I hugged him.

"Daddy went home that day. That day Daddy saw Jesus face-to-face. We were all in tears. We were all in need of the Lord's comfort. The funeral was on New Year's Eve. At midnight, in my parent's backyard, we released white balloons with messages written in love up to heaven. Kind of my way of writing letters back to my dad."

Isabella grabbed a tissue to dab the tears from her eyes. "Thanks, everyone, for listening. Getting choked up, but that's okay, right? God is good, and it's only by His strength that I stand before you to offer hope." The audience clapped for Isabella with shouts of encouragement to continue.

"In my search for answers, my soul found hope in the book of Jeremiah, which speaks of calling out to God while believing He will answer. I hold on tightly to that scripture to this day. Courage began to grow, and I soon found myself developing a desire to work in pulmonary medicine. Dad knew I was going to apply for an internship abroad. I wish he could see that my dream came true. Wish he knew that I still have the letters. I brought some letters here with me. I believe it was meant to happen that way.

"I stand before you as someone who is said to have experienced a medical miracle. I stand before you as someone who came out of denial. I stand before you as someone who is holding tight to the Lord. I stand before you as someone who wants to tell others that even though you may not be able to relate to my story, we have something in common. I can relate to pain. I stand before you as someone who is thankful for taking the step to seek healing through recovery ministries."

Like a flame's first flicker that precedes a roaring fire, so was the first glimpse of healing into Isabella's soul. Instantly a word picture came to her mind. She was brought back to the first night the wrought iron table became her special place. The place where tears flowed. The place where God was felt. The place where her heart broke into pieces, allowing God's light to shine through the cracks. Now those cracks had been filled with transparent sealant, a sealant that would keep it from falling apart while the cracks remained visible. Isabella knew now that those cracks were all part of her story of redemption, healing, and grace. That day there was abounding hope deep inside that was more powerful than she had ever known.

"After I truly surrendered any pride and fear, let walls down, and came face-to-face with the recovery process of openly examining my life, admitting and confessing any faults, offering forgiveness, and making amends, change began to take place. This level of transparency was new to me. Soon, with the Lord on my side, I was able to break the ice and let true healing come in. I sensed the Lord near. It was then that I started to believe that my life, my story, has purpose.

"What's your story? Yes, your story. Each of you has a story. Each of you has a purpose. As I was writing my testimony last night, I thought about that question a lot. The word 'what' inspires and challenges me to look at life and ask what God has placed in my hands to accomplish, in my relationships, my ministry outreach, my workplace, and so on. Then I considered whether I had thanked Him recently for those 'what' elements. I challenge you all to look within and ask yourselves the same question. What has God placed in your hands? Do you know He did so because He thought you were the best one for that purpose? Have you thanked Him?"

Holy Spirit, there's no way I could be standing here without your help. There's just no way. I know you entered this place. In that public setting, Isabella was having a private moment of internal dialogue from deep within, giving thanks for what she believed was divine intervention. She felt courage. She felt humbled. She felt inner peace. Whenever Isabella talked about God moving in her life, she became very animated and used her hands for emphasis. The animation continued as she asked a few volunteers to hand out a piece of paper to everyone.

"The blank page before you is just that: a blank page. There's wonder in a blank page, isn't there? So many possibilities of what could be written on it. Anything at all. My hope is that you will spend some time this evening writing out your story. Your testimony is powerful, and it has purpose. Be encouraged that God is the author and finisher of our faith. Will you trust that His plans are perfect? He is the One who guides our steps. He is the One who loves us with an everlasting love, and He is the One writing your story."

Isabella had a flashback to the moment of sitting on the den floor with her new loose-leaf paper, pencil case, and blue three-ring binder. She remembered telling her parents how excited she was to start sixth grade. "I wonder what you'll write on those pages, sweetheart." Her mom would say those words at the beginning of every school year. Quickly looking up at her mom seated in the front row, Isabella felt tremendous gratitude. Right then her mom winked and nodded. Isabella smiled and winked back—a sweet moment indeed. Refocusing, she continued.

"With each day we should seek to have a positive effect on the lives of others. Our smile may be the only smile someone sees. Our hug may be the only hug a person feels. Our sharing God's words of hope and truth may be the only words others hear about Him. We need to ask others about their hopes. We need to ask how we can pray for them, and if they say they don't have any prayer requests, we need to pray even more. Our life really isn't about focusing on just us, right? It's about being a light to others in His name.

"Something amazing happens when we take our eyes off of ourselves. That is surely one of the ingredients in the recipe of a rich life. Ask questions, build friendships, ignite conversations, and most importantly, get to know God and His character by reading His story. What are your hopes? When was the last time you even asked yourself that question? Do you have any hopes?"

The room was silent. All eyes were focused on Isabella. Everyone was being inspired. Everyone was being challenged. Isabella could see it. She could feel it. She was healing.

"Now, looking at the word 'story', my heart is encouraged that God isn't finished writing my story. He's not finished writing your story either. The challenging question for us all is whether we will allow Him to write chapters in our lives even if those chapters are difficult. During those trying pages, will we have the same love for Him as we would if those same chapters were filled with love, blessings, and excitement? What a dynamic challenge, because once a chapter or two or three has been written, we have the unique opportunity to turn back the pages and read what God wrote. Trust in Him. Trust His plan. Get excited! Look forward with great anticipation to turning the pages of your story! Thank you all for letting me share. God bless."

Everyone stood up, clapping, crying, cheering, and acknowledging Isabella for her bravery. It was a moment she would never forget and knew the Lord had ordained. All that she had gone through had led up to this very moment. All the good, all the joyful, all the hurt, and all the pain had all been for Him. Her light was shining brightly. With deep passion for Christ and a desire for others to find the same hope, Isabella knew she would press on. She had found purpose in her pain. A secret now revealed only after her mask was removed. Isabella's vision, her calling, had come full circle. Oh yes, that light was shining.

The Beginning

CPSIA information can be obtained
at www.ICGtesting.com
Printed in the USA
BVHW080945080519
547715BV00004B/425/P